THE DESERTER

THE
DESERTER

Giuseppe Dessí

*Translated from
the Italian by*
VIRGINIA HATHAWAY MORICONI

A Helen and Kurt Wolff Book
Harcourt, Brace & World, Inc./New York

THE DESERTER

1

When they first began talking of the monument Mariangela Eca had no inkling of what it was all about. Her
two sons had been dead for more than four years but
for her it was as if no time had gone by at all.

For everyone else in Cuadu, including those who had
lost a son, a nephew, or a husband, the end of the war
was already far away, so many, so profound were the
changes that the war and the postwar years had brought,
even to that small town. But not for Mariangela. She was
no longer aware of what was happening around her and
the world still seemed what it had been when her sons
were growing up and pasturing their herds of goats in
the Baddimanna woods and making cheese and ricotta in
the old sheepfold. Cuadu, the whole world, or at least
all she could imagine of it, was just as it was when they
had left her to weep for them. They had gone away and
left her behind with their father, who had grown old and
feeble, and with the wife of Saverio, the elder, and from
that moment everything had ceased to matter but the
past. Week in, week out, she continued to live, to make
her daily rounds, to bring down from Baddimanna the
heavy bundles of wood that she sold for twenty-five
centesimi as before the war, but it was only the past that
counted. She remembered the world as it was when the
two boys were beginning to make their own way in it
and start their families.

The parish priest of Cuadu, Don Pietro Coi, was her neighbor. She had been doing his housework for twenty years. Don Pietro never stopped trying to make her understand how difficult life had become for all of them, to make her see that everything was changed in fact. The war had been a great disaster, not only for her but for everyone. Millions of men had left their homes behind them, millions of men in all countries, and afterwards new calamities afflicted all mankind.

As he spoke to her of these things the priest hoped, if not to comfort her, at least to distract her for a little from the closed and fixed idea of her own suffering. But in his heart he knew that the old woman could find no relief from pain in the sufferings of others, through abstract meditation on the suffering of the world. If he insisted it was partly that the habit of his profession was to comfort and admonish, and partly because he himself was moved by that silent, definitive grief.

He began to find fault with her, to scold her. A trifle was enough to make him lose his temper. But the real reason for this was that he could not find words that seemed to him adequate, or even acceptable. For all the daily intimacy of those years, for all that he constantly reminded her that it was her duty to resign herself, to bow to the Lord's will, she was unshakable. In silence she went on bustling about. It made no difference if he were angry or if, patient and paternal, he reasoned with her. Sometimes he would make her stop working to bring

4

her to task. Then she stood before him like a schoolgirl with her head bent, looking at his shoes.

So it continued, although he was wiser to the sufferings of Mariangela than to the suffering of any other woman in Cuadu, wife, sister, or mother of a soldier fallen in the war. Reproaching her for her lack of resignation, of humility, reminding her that she was not the only one who had suffered, he would allude to all the other women whose sorrows he had understood, whom he had had to comfort, one by one. The first time he spoke of them Mariangela had appeared to be shocked from her habitual listlessness for a moment. She had lifted her tearless eyes to his face as if to convince herself that he had indeed said what she had heard, which seemed so strange to her.

Among the women in mourning was her daughter-in-law, Lica, who had been the wife of Saverio, her elder son. Like many other war widows she was living with another man, but out of wedlock, in order not to lose her husband's pension. Privately Don Pietro found it just that Mariangela might wonder at a likeness between her grieving and a grieving that could be comforted, even come to an end. The next time he referred only to the mothers who had been bereaved, but once again he saw the old woman's eyes searching his face and once more, in his heart, he justified her disbelief and her astonishment. Thereafter he could not rouse her at all, not even with that argument that he had chosen deliberately.

5

The truth was that for everyone else, including the mothers in mourning, the life of the present, however squalid, mattered more than remembrance, although none of them was willing to admit such a thing out loud. The life of the present, which day by day one has to live. In one way or another everyone had found consolation, had come to sort out the memories of the past, to confine them within proper limits from which they did not escape. This, said the priest, was part of the logic of things that coincides with the mystery of divine will. No matter how profound were the sufferings of those mothers, no matter how deeply, in the first moments, each one rebelled at the knowledge that her own life must continue beyond that of her lost son, over the years this maternal rebellion was, in most cases, controlled and dominated, if not overcome, through a nicer discrimination in thinking, in which memory and longing found peace in prayers which came to be recited at specific hours of the day, and on certain special days that recurred each year and were recognized, generally. Thus the grieving, guarded in secret, became a public, even a national thing, and as such directly useful to the country. All the same it was not less felt. Indeed it was the only way to remind people of it, to make it solemnly endure, to perpetuate it.

Mariangela's grief, instead, remained private. Once, on the occasion of a public celebration (the first time she had gone, not knowing what it was all about), as the mayor of Cuadu was in the act of extolling the sublime sentiments that had led so many mothers to offer their sons to the Patria, Mariangela, who found herself in the front row, as the mother of two sons, both casualties, with the two military crosses that she had just pinned to her black shawl, Mariangela had uttered, in a loud voice, a word that left the first citizen literally paralyzed. The word was clearly heard by everyone close to her, but nevertheless no one could be certain that it was she who had said it.

No one, that is, except Don Pietro. There she stood, wrapped in her black shawl, her hands clasped across her womb, her head cocked to one side, absorbed in her thoughts, apparently incapable of understanding, let alone uttering, such an obscenity in that solemn moment.

Only Don Pietro knew that it was she, but he kept it to himself and never reproached her for it. He knew, because once she had answered him in the same way, and then too she had been absorbed in herself and had hardly raised an eyebrow.

She had said it as he was trying to persuade her that the death of the two boys had not been in vain or unmerciful, as she believed.

Even that time he had held his peace, as if nothing had happened.

2

Since no one would admit that her sons had died for nothing Mariangela preferred not to hear them spoken of, and she herself never spoke of them, not even to Don Pietro, except in confession. This normally came about once a year, at Easter. Outside of that, although she knew what he was thinking, his exhortations and reproaches went unanswered, as if she found them merely passing humors.

In certain periods of the year whole weeks passed in which they did not exchange a single word except for "The Lord be praised," with which, quiet as a mouse, she announced that she had arrived, or that she was about to leave. In silence she swept, did the dishes, cooked, washed, ironed without a change of expression. She could prolong these silences indefinitely. In the long run the priest would lose his patience and find some pretext to scold her. He overworked her, shouted at her, let himself go with her, but whatever the provocation, in the end he returned to the same old saw, her lack of resignation, and there he laid the blame for the unstarched collars and the unpolished shoes. Mariangela let him talk, but those were the only moments when a flash of sympathy or indulgence crossed her face.

Nor did the priest grow accustomed, with the years' passing, to the silent, immutable grief that had descended on her, and often her presence disturbed him to the point of preventing him from concentrating on his reading, or his prayers. He wound up by scolding her, while he waited impatiently for her to go. What a relief it was when he heard the garden gate close behind her. She would not be back until the next day. He had even begun seriously to think of letting her go. But it was not easy, since Mariangela and her husband were neighbors, the gardens bordered on each other, and she had been doing his housework since her son, Saverio, had had worms when he was ten years old.

Don Pietro, prodded by Mariangela, had recited certain magical verses, although he himself had put no faith in them, and the child was cured. Then Mariangela had offered to work for him. Obstinately she had almost imposed herself on him, partly from gratitude and partly, as he perfectly recognized, from superstition— as if being in and out of his house and waiting on him were a means, not so much to avail herself of the mysterious powers she attributed to him, as to neutralize them. The plain proof of this was that she had never been willing to accept his money in payment. Don Pietro had insisted in vain. In the end he had set up a postal savings account for her where, each month, he deposited the salary that he had fixed, one scudo.

Five lire then was a just wage for her modest services, perhaps even excessive, but later, with the gradual devaluation of the currency, it no longer seemed to him sufficient. Nevertheless each month he continued to deposit the usual five lire in the savings account as a gesture, while promising himself over and over that, at some opportune moment, he would add the difference all at once.

Since that distant time roughly eight hundred lire had accumulated in the account, but in fourteen years Mariangela had never spoken of the sum, although she knew of its existence. So the priest was in no small way astonished when one day she asked him if the money were still there, and if she could use it as she pleased, and he was the more astonished when she went on to ask if he could give it to her. Don Pietro, who happened to have such a sum in the house, went and took it out of the desk drawer and gave it to her immediately, without any question, certain that later on she would tell him what she wanted it for. The money was in silver and a number of notes. Mariangela counted them, wrapped them up in a handkerchief and, under his eye, which was following each motion, she put them in the deep pocket of her skirt where she kept her rosary and the little knife she took to cut her bread when she went up into the hills. He understood that the money had a particular destination, but she said nothing, not that day nor any of the days that followed. It was this lack of explanation that aroused his first suspicions.

Just at that time small groups of girls, organized by the Marchese Roberto Manca di Tharros, were beginning to go from house to house asking a few cents from the poor for the monument that was to be raised in the main square of Cuadu. They went as they had gone in time of war, when they were collecting funds for the Red Cross, with a tricolored ribbon pinned to their sleeves, and empty shoeboxes, sealed with sealing wax, in which they had cut slits with a penknife for coins or bills. Don Pietro suspected something as soon as he saw the girls, but he pulled himself up short at once, thinking how far it would be from Mariangela to yield to the promptings of those schoolteachers, those propagandists who were always talking of the Patria, of the holocaust, of maternal heroism—all the things that had made her speak that word. But shortly thereafter his intuition was confirmed.

He was going by the Piazza when Roberto Manca, who was holding a meeting of sorts at the door of the Society, called out to him in a loud voice, waving a piece of paper that was, as he later learned, a letter of thanks for Mariangela. Manca was declaiming that the poor had set an example for the rich, that a poor woman who earned her meager living either as an underpaid servant or by selling bundles of wood, who had given both her sons for Italy, was now offering her mite for the erection of the monument—eight hundred and thirty-five lire, a figure that not even the most well-to-do had dreamed of giving.

"And this woman," he cried, red in the face, with the veins bursting out on his neck, "this woman is your servant, Father Coi, your servant!"

Everyone in Cuadu knew that Don Pietro had been against Captain Manca and his project from the beginning. He had spoken his mind wherever he went, maintaining that all that was needed to commemorate their dead was a plaque, fastened to the façade of the Town Hall. Wasn't it ridiculous to spend so much money for a monument, which would be ugly, without doubt, when there were so many other things urgently needed in Cuadu? Here the priest, through these arguments, which Manca labeled "defeatist," found himself aligned with the wealthiest citizens, the "prinzipales" who opposed the project because they were afraid that an eventual appropriation of funds by the town administration would mean an increase in taxes. And it was on this account that the noble Roberto Manca, captain of the auxiliary forces, decorated for valor, wounded, even invalided with a pension, unself-sparing volunteer and, as Father Coi said, an "honorary casualty," cried out against him from the door of the Society, waving his piece of paper. Unfortunately, Manca could never let himself go like that with Commendatore Alessandro Comina, his most forceful adversary.

3

_____

With such an airing no one in Cuadu talked of anything else. The story of Mariangela Eca's eight hundred lire went the rounds of every house. They talked about it at the Society, the Post Office, the Town Hall, in the shops, the barbershops, by the public washtubs, and in the sacristy. Everyone had his own comment to make and the most far-fetched hypotheses were advanced. Some even insinuated that Mariangela had not made her offering without her employer's knowledge, or against his will, but by his own suggestion, with his connivance— precisely because Father Coi wished to amuse himself by embarrassing the Committee. This absurd supposition gained ground and was generally accepted even by the priest's supporters, who were laughing on the sly while they admired the extraordinary finesse of the dodge.

It did seem strange that a poor woman like Mariangela could dispose of such a considerable amount of money and, admitting that she could, it seemed equally strange that it should have come into her mind thus to disburden herself for a monument to the dead, even taking into account that two of these were her own sons. With eight hundred lire she could, like other people, have built a private monument in the cemetery. Still, this odd version of the facts was finally accepted both by the friends of Don Pietro and by the partisans of the Marchese.

Among the latter was the Monsignor, Tarcisio Pau, who, as the representative of the Archdiocese, was a member of the Committee. Only a few days before he had recommended that, after the reading of the Gospel, Don Pietro explain the meaning of the monument to the faithful. To which his subordinate replied that he would do such a thing only if it were an order. If it were not an order—and most irregular—but a simple request, he preferred to direct his attention, and the attention of the faithful, to other subjects. Dryly the Monsignor had replied that, as of that instant, the request had become an order, and Don Pietro, who could do no less, had bowed his head and had explained from the altar, that Sunday, the "Purpose of the Committee."

Well-informed persons said that Monsignor Tarcisio Pau might have been one of the youngest bishops in the Church were the prospective appointment not always under fire and later postponed on account of his rash and stormy character. In retaliation, he asserted himself in a feverish activity that extended even to politics. Graduate in law as well as in theology, he had completed his studies at one of the best-known academies in the capital and had been chaplain to a general of the army—something that had enormously increased his prestige and made him an authoritative despot.

Don Pietro Coi, elderly and without ambition, rough, sardonic, neglectful of his person, constantly gave the young Monsignor grounds for complaint and reproach, but as a rule he bore with him patiently. It was only once in a while that he turned on his hot-tempered superior. The Monsignor, for his part, knew perfectly well when this patience was wearing thin, when it would have been perilous to utter one more syllable. Don Pietro's greatest sacrifice had been made at the beginning when, arriving in Cuadu, and newly invested with all his authority as Vicar, the Monsignor had prevailed on him to stop hunting.

One day, after Mariangela's offering and the petty gossip that was going about, the Monsignor greeted him with a sarcastic little laugh. It was marvelous, he said, to think what a fortune Don Pietro would spend just for spite—and he was buzzing like a wasp as he fitted onto his head the "nicchio," which tended to fly off, like a black butterfly.

He was in the sacristy, dressing himself for the Mass with the help of the seminarian and the altar boys. Don Pietro stood at the door with his hat in his hand. The Monsignor was ill-natured but he was hardly stupid. "Not to such a point as this," thought Don Pietro, laying his hat in its usual place, on top of the wardrobe.

Now this trick of putting his hat on the wardrobe was something that the Monsignor could not endure. Being short and plethoric himself, it struck him that the priest, who was tall and thin, was simply showing off. Don Pietro, on the other hand, was only doing as he invariably did; he found it the most natural place for his hat. This time Monsignor Pau sensed something of the priest's surprise, in that gesture, and it irritated him more than ever, constrained as he was to raise his short, fat arms so that his assistants could tie the tapes of his vestments.

"So it's really true, he's stupid," thought Don Pietro,

and considered him with some amusement, slowly shaking his head.

This reflection was written so clearly on his face that the Monsignor could think of nothing whatsoever to say, and furiously he put on the surplice which the seminarian was holding out for him.

4

When she gave her money to the schoolteacher, Pietrina Cherchi, Mariangela had no notion of the consequences, of the debates to follow, much less could she have foreseen that Don Pietro might find himself in an embarrassing position on her account. In good faith she thought of it as a matter only between herself and the teacher. She was quite well aware that the sum was considerable. Poor as she was, and reckoning the currency as it had been before the war when the silver scudo of Vittorio Emanuele the Second was still in circulation, and even an occasional marengo, she found it an enormous amount of money. For precisely that reason she had counted on the schoolteacher's discretion. Why should she talk? It was just between the two of them. Were other women expected to tell what they slipped through the crack in the shoebox? She had given the money away without even untying the ends of the handkerchief, which she had knotted under Father Coi's scrutiny. And the teacher had taken it as if for granted, without a word. Or had she mistaken it for eggs? Every so often she used to bring her half a dozen fresh eggs. That was what the teacher must have thought when she herself had gone away without giving her time to see what was wrapped up inside the handkerchief. In any case she could not have imagined that for days and days no one in Cuadu would talk about anything else. Just as she had not felt that she was making a sacrifice, or depriving herself of something important.

The money simply did not belong to her, according to her way of thinking. It belonged neither to her nor to anyone else. Not even to Don Pietro. Not that it was in jest that the priest had opened the savings account for her fourteen years ago, but neither was it in jest the promise that she had made to herself to work for him without pay. It was a vow that she had taken privately, after the miraculous disappearance of Saverio's worms.

It was true that the priest had not wished to accept her services for nothing, and it was equally true that in all those years she had never touched a single lira of the stipend that he had put aside for her, against her will—never, not so much as a lira, for fear of turning against her sons the indefinable power that emanated from the priest and from that house to which she went with reverent dread, that house which stood wall to wall with her own. That money, which the obstinate Don Pietro deposited, year after year, would have been left at the

Post Office indefinitely, she would never had touched it if Giovanni and Saverio had been still alive. It would have stayed there forever—or perhaps she might have asked the priest to give it to the Church, or to charity, after her death. But for herself she would not have taken a lira, not even to buy bread if she were starving.

So long as her sons were alive that money, deposited, and almost suspended at an equal distance between herself and Don Pietro, had a reason for being, and a reason for remaining where it was. She could forget about it. But in the four years since the boys had died she worried about it all the time. What was she to do with it? It was an encumbrance when she thought of it, an anxiety, an obsession. Thus when she heard them talk about the monument and they explained to her that the names of her own sons would be written on it, carved into the stone together with the names of all the other young men of Cuadu who had been killed in the war, she saw it as the best way to rid herself of a dead weight.

Everything they said was more and more convincing. Moreover, the monument itself seemed to her the final contradiction of all the words that she hated, about the Patria and the holocaust. She knew that the names would be written on its face, and nothing else. The monument would be silent. It would be the end of all the discussions, all the nonsense that they kept repeating about the dead.

She had had this idea thinking, perhaps, of the few

marble gravestones in the Cuadu cemetery, isolated between the simple iron and wooden crosses, stones that both dominated the silence and seemed to emanate silence.

Thus a vision of the monument had taken shape in her mind. For the first time, thanks to this symbol, her own suffering found comfort in the sufferings of others—a comfort that no words had ever been able to give her.

Her conception of it was already fixed when Don Pietro, breaking the reserve that he had imposed on himself, scolded her for the offering of eight hundred and thirty-five lire.

5

———————

It happened in Father Coi's garden, one afternoon. He was pruning a rosebush when he heard the creak of the wooden gate and, turning, he saw her going into the house with the basket of linen that she had ironed.

At the sight of her he was shaken with rage but, cutting off two or three other twigs, he had time to calm himself. He breathed deeply, closed the scissors, and continued to smooth the wounded branch with the grafting knife until he heard the rustle of bare feet behind him, steps coming nearer. He turned slowly and considered her at his leisure—so old, small, thin, with the black scarf and apron of her perpetual mourning gone greenish from the sun and the rain.

That was what she looked like.

Although Mariangela came every day to do his chores, once she had gone he always forgot how she had changed, and he would find fault with her. Scolding her in his mind, he thought of her as she had been many years ago when she was still young. She had been small, but she was strong, wiry, stubborn, her eyes alive and ironic in the silence, and there was a sly twist to her lip that gave her an expression of particular cunning. Small and strong she had been.

The priest took his eyes off her, blew furiously on the pruning shears, which he was still holding, fastened the leather strap meticulously, and, bending forward a little from the knee—until a few years before he had worn hunting socks and high boots under his vestments—he put the shears deep in his side pocket. After which he spoke, lifting his huge, broad hand against her.

"You shouldn't have given anything to that woman," he said, brusquely.

With a snap he opened the grafting knife and began to smooth the torn branch again with the blade.

"You shouldn't have given her anything, not a lira!"

He turned to look at her. She stood there without answering, her head bent. "Nothing!" he said. He was aware that he was almost shouting.

For an instant her eyes glittered maliciously as she tucked her hair under her scarf.

"Eight hundred lire!" he exclaimed, with a deprecating gesture.

He fished the pruning shears out of his pocket and twirled them in the air. Then in one neat, precise stroke he cut another twig from the delicate, slightly misshapen bush with its slender branches, its trembling leaves. Meanwhile he was asking himself, "But what's eight hundred lire, after all?"

She kept her eyes on the ground, now considering the twigs cut from the bush, now the priest's muddy shoes.

"You're a poor woman," he said, and cleared his throat. "No one else gave such a lot of money. How much do you think Commendatore Comina gave, for instance? And yet even he—"

He had been about to say, "Even he had a son killed in the war," but he stopped himself in time.

She stretched her neck without answering a word, just as she always did when she was scolded. There was an odor of smoke about her—of smoke in a hovel, he thought, with a sense of distaste, and of pity.

"And your husband? Your husband said nothing to you?"

She shrugged her shoulders lightly, like a schoolgirl.

The priest blew on the shears and slipped them into his pocket again. Seeing that he had finished pruning the bush, the woman bent swiftly to pick up the fallen twigs, gathered them in her apron, and went to throw them on the heap of dried leaves beside the hedge.

"You did it for spite," he said. "For spite." And he

glanced once more at her crooked, bony back before he strode off toward the house. She caught up with him, trotting rapidly, and they went together into the kitchen.

"Could you tell me how much you get for a bundle of wood?" he said, stopping in the middle of the room and looking at her.

His head bumped against the light that hung from the ceiling. He steadied it and slid down the counterweight, to raise it. Then he closed his eyes and murmured to himself, "Oh, Lord."

"It takes a whole day to gather a bundle of wood," he said, almost in a whisper. He pointed his finger at the wall, in the direction of the mountain. "You go all the way up there—"

In his mind's eye he saw the bare open space at Baddimanna and the sheepfold where he used to stop and drink a cup of fresh milk when he went hunting. He saw the great shed with its triangular door. Very slowly he lowered his arm. He sat down, he bent to untie his shoes. Without saying a word the woman went to get the clean shoes from behind the stove and knelt to help him put them on, as she always did, but he pushed her hands away rudely. Her silence irritated him more than ever—that silence born, ripened, and grown old within herself, that earthy, uninstructed silence.

"You're old, you and Girolamo," said the priest. "You should think of the future. Who'll give you money when you can't work any more? You'll go begging."

She shook her head and sighed. With her eyes still

fixed on one corner of the room she pulled herself up wearily and went to fetch the tin of roasted coffee and the mill. All at once the racket of the grinder filled the kitchen. She was hugging it to her breast and staring out the window, enveloped and protected by the noise.

6

From long habit Don Pietro Coi was accustomed to read people's thoughts—the simplest thoughts, which could not be put into words. He had always read Mariangela's. Sometimes, on account of her impassiveness, he understood them a little late; however, he knew them. During those years of remarkable silence he kept coming up against them, rediscovering them. But now, underlying that constant, if unspoken, harping on her sons, there was something more obscure within her that he failed to grasp, something impenetrable, a silence inside the silence.

Don Pietro had seen her anguish when the Carabinieri brought her the first telegram announcing the death of Giovanni, her younger son. Suffering can be transparent, like joy. But when, after some months, Saverio, the survivor, was reported missing, an abyss of silence had separated Mariangela from the rest of the world, an unvoiced, tearless agony that had lasted. She had ceased to complain. She had given one cry and then she had set herself at the window, looking out, exactly as she was doing now.

Thus even when he was able to read her thoughts, penetrate her secrets, and understand them, his comprehension served for nothing, except perhaps for a certain solidarity, since the silence was shared between them. If for a moment, presuming on a flash of sympathy, he tried to reach her, to speak to her, then the silence became impenetrable; it was as if sorrow had carried her away, leaving an empty shape. Absently she stared at his shoes, and if at a certain point she recovered herself and looked him in the face, it was a mute prayer for silence.

After that single cry she had wept only once. It was when, a few days later, he was explaining to her that "missing" did not mean "dead"—Saverio might still come home. The old woman had bitten her lips, lifted her eyes to his, looked at him searchingly, and then those eyes had filled with tears. How miserable and inept he had felt, at that moment!

Saverio had been given a furlough, after the death of his younger brother. The Company Commander had let him hope that he might be discharged from military service. But since by the end of his leave that hope, which his mother took as a promise, had not been realized, he had gone back to the front. Then the news had come. Missing. They had not had the courage to tell her that he was dead, that was what she thought, and she had given that barking cry.

For her the news was final. Not for an instant did she let herself believe that her son might be alive, really alive, as Don Pietro said, although he doubted it himself. It never crossed her mind that then, just at that moment, he might be journeying through a thousand difficulties and perils, that he might be trying to get back to Cuadu, to hide himself in the woods of Baddimanna which he knew, tree for tree, and gorge for gorge, where, until two years before, he had brought his goats to pasture every night. She could not have imagined that a month from that day she was to see him again—after she had believed him surely dead, abandoned in a ditch, picked clean by birds and ants (she had no notion of the front, of the trenches, of the barbed wire, although Saverio had tried to explain to her how it was, nor of what happened to the dead, out there)—that she was to see him alive, at the door of the old deserted sheepfold, with his strong, primitive smell of a man, of a shepherd.

But that was three years ago and Saverio had died. Time went on, all other persuasions were useless, and Don Pietro could do nothing but scold her. He was harsh, but his attitude only reflected his uneasiness in the face of a confusion that derived from something unresolved between himself and the old woman.

Often he asked himself if possibly Mariangela did not feel responsible for the death of her son. Perhaps she believed that it was she who had put the idea of flight into his head when, childishly, foolishly, she had made him promise to escape, to save himself. Afterward she might have felt guilty, taken on herself the blame for his crazy flight, because she had pleaded with him absurdly, at the moment of parting.

Although Mariangela had confessed nothing of the sort, he had arrived at a near certainty that she blamed herself for what had happened. She was ignorant of the truth, but only the priest knew that. Many times, especially at first, he had been on the point of telling her the facts, but he had put temptation aside. He had no right to make her part of a secret that had been entrusted to himself and must die with himself alone. There was no hope at all of tearing her from her fixed and immutable reflections.

7

_____

Mariangela had put the coffeepot on the stove, over the coals. While she waited for the water to come to a boil she kept looking at the corner of the window, instinctively moving her head, from time to time, as if she were swallowing. She could bide her time indefinitely, without answering the questions that were put to her, and within her was neither arrogance nor embarrassment, but an ancient, subtle persuasion of silence. Sometimes, after long intervals, she spoke of her sons to Don Pietro, but only in confession, because the confessional is also a silence, a silence where one communicates almost without words, a deep, deep silence from which an echo returns, and then dies.

When the water began to spit from the little hole near the spout, Mariangela turned the coffeepot upside down quickly, dried it with a cloth, and put it by Don Pietro. The coffee filtered down drop by drop with a precise *toc, toc*, spreading its essence through the room.

"Take a cup for yourself too," said the priest.

She brought a cup but no saucer for herself, and put it beside his. Small and dry, her sparse pepper-and-salt hair parted in the middle of her head and half covered with the greenish scarf that had once been black, she seemed older than she was, and there was that odor of smoke about her, of a hovel filled with smoke, and of old silence. The priest poured the coffee in both cups, nodded, and she took hers. She was just the same age as he, but she looked much older.

While she sipped the coffee he was watching her. She blew on it before each swallow. He always needed to look at her to convince himself of how old she had grown, to remind himself that she was no longer strong as she was before the death of her sons. He thought of her still as she had been, many years before, when her sons were little—Giovanni, the robust one, the bully, and Saverio, thin and sickly. He had agreed, half seriously, half laughing at himself, to recite those strange verses (they

27

were then in the Breviary!), and the child really had
been cured of worms in a single night. Mariangela had
come racing to tell him about it, dragging the reluctant
boy behind her, and she had kissed his hand, which was
not usual for her. Then her hair was black, she was
strong—a small, strong, inexhaustible woman, capable
of carrying enormous weights on her head. Even then she
had had that odor of smoke about her, the odor of the
poor of Cuadu, and that stubbornness.

"No, I don't need anything else," said the priest, in
answer to the old woman's questioning gesture, and she
took her leave, saying, as always, "Jesus Christ be
praised," to which Don Pietro replied, making the sign
of the Cross with two fingers and just moving his lips,
"Let Him be praised forever."

8

The proposal to erect, in Cuadu, a monument to the
dead of the Great War had been put forward almost a
year ago by Roberto Manca di Tharros, but the gentle-
men of the Queen Margherita Literary Society had let
it slide. It was at the Society that the most important
questions of the citizenry were decided. The members
weighed, evaluated, and examined beforehand all the
resolutions that the Town Council had to consider, and

the Society was made up of the Cuadu aristocracy, and of the sons, grandsons, and friends of the members.

The mayor, at that time, was Edmondo Escano, a poor man's son. As a boy he had swept the clubhouse floors or fetched the shotguns for Dante Tavèra or the Isalle brothers, when they went hunting, and it was then that his left hand was maimed. Later he had been taken under contract as Steward of the Smoking Room, but since he was a good shot and clever at cards, he shortly became a sort of administrator, or superintendent of the Society, which was literary in name only. In fact it was a club for gamblers and sportsmen, the place where the "prinzipales" of Cuadu could escape from their wives and spend their most pleasurable hours playing cards, smoking, and drinking vernaccia or acquavit, which Edmondo furnished, along with the cards and the tobacco.

There was, however, a reading room, real and proper, with a large table covered by an old cloth, a dozen armchairs, some newspapers, and a portrait of the Queen Mother, which harked back to the times of "La Bella Otero." But people were used to reading more, in those days, if the empty racks on the walls were anything to go by. After the war, both for economy and for prudence, the number of subscriptions had been reduced. There were four or five daily papers, some published on the island, including the organ of the separatist party, a bellicose sheet that several of the members considered downright revolutionary, on account of its attacks on the country and its government, but which most of the rest of them accepted with certain reservations.

With all that was going on in the Peninsula, the islanders' best bet—so ran the editorials—was secession, once and for all, from Italy proper, and the consequent transformation of a former handicap into a present advantage. With independence, it went on to say, commerce might be resumed with France. Heated discussions arose in the reading room over this proposal, although it was almost always the old ones who read about or argued politics. The young bloods went on playing in the next room, and if they ever gathered at the door it was only to enjoy the spectacle of someone beating his fists on the table and shouting. Even then there were always a handful of dauntless players who went on playing scopone or tresette, not bothering themselves with what was happening in the other room. Edmondo was one of these. After the first hand he knew how the cards lay, which was all he cared about, or so it seemed.

When Roberto Manca put forward the first proposal for the monument, Edmondo had just been elected mayor —through the influence of Commendatore Alessandro Comina, it was said, although no one knew that for certain since, in all such matters, the Steward of the Smoking Room behaved just as he did at the card table, lighting one cigarette after another, not saying a word.

By that time the Cominas had become far more important than the Mancas. The Marchesi Manca di Tharros had been powerful in the past, but things had changed, the grass had grown under their feet. As far as the land went, they held the same number of acres as when they had been one of the wealthiest families in Cuadu—and wealthy since the beginning—but those acres had lain fallow and were not worth what they had been when they were pasture for hundreds of wild sheep and goats and cows. Roberto had gone off to fight and his mother, Antonietta Manca, had managed the estate, but she was very old. What small amount of money the land had yielded during the war—small in view of what it might have been made to yield—became, with the devaluation of the currency, no more than scrap paper in no time at all.

Affairs had taken quite a different turn for the Cominas, on the other hand. Even before the war they had built a soap factory, a tannery, a distillery, and two flour mills, and the huge war profits had been advantageously invested. They had not gone to fight. Or rather Alessandro's youngest son, Benigno, had gone, against his father's wishes, a volunteer like Roberto Manca, and he had fallen at Doberdò. In the Cuadu cemetery there was a tombstone with his photograph and an empty grave, because the body had not been recovered. Wealth, increased tenfold, and this dead son—of whom he never spoke and of whom no one, not even the members of the family, dared remind him—conferred an incontestable authority on old Alessandro Comina.

When the body of the Unknown Soldier was brought down to Rome from the Carso, Roberto Manca had been part of the honorary escort. Shortly thereafter he had proposed to establish a committee for the erection of a monument to the dead of Cuadu, addressing himself, with due respect, to old Comina. The Commendatore had struck the table with the newspaper rack and, shouting something incomprehensible, had walked out.

In the uneasy silence that followed everyone was thinking of the old grudges between the Mancas and the Cominas. In all likelihood they would come to open, irremediable dissension, or even worse, there, on the spot, because, among the incomprehensible words that the Commendatore had shouted, one had come across to all of them—*blockhead*.

Roberto, pale as death, had risen slowly and was on the point of rushing after the old man who had already left, leaning on his stout cane, his limp as fierce and vigorous as ever, still shouting and gesticulating even when he reached the middle of the Piazza.

But in the meantime his eldest son, Gino, had not lost his composure. Pale himself, he had gone over to Roberto and, in the general silence, had apologized for his father.

It had had to be done, there was nothing else to do, yet no one was expecting it, least of all Roberto. For a moment he hesitated. He ran his hands through his hair and looked from one to another. The offense was grave and concerned not only himself but the cause he was pleading, the monument, and all that the monument symbolized.

It was clear to everyone what old Comina thought of war, of the Patria, of the sacrifice of those who had gone to fight and had fallen, or come home wounded, disabled, covered with medals. It was clear what he thought of the Fiume Expedition, of the Legionaries, and of D'Annunzio—"he's a fool, like all the others"—and it was clear that the Queen Margherita Literary Society subscribed to the newspaper of the separatist party because the Commendatore wished it. All this was common knowledge, which made the injury far graver.

Nobody spoke. Distinctly one could hear the breathing of those present, the creak of a chair, the deliberate, peremptory smack of the cards that came from the adjoining room, where Edmondo and two or three others were still playing.

"I beg you to excuse my father," repeated Gino Comina. His short blond mustache was trembling over his pale tight lips. Roberto remembered the photograph of Gino's dead brother. He thought of it indifferently for a moment while Gino waited, his head slightly cocked, like a boxer's after a round, then suddenly, without a word, they fell into each other's arms. There was a burst of applause. The two of them, embracing, were by this time really moved, the one clapping the other on the shoulder or patting the back of his neck with fine, strong, aristocratic hands. Vernaccia and acquavit were brought by Edmondo, everyone drank a toast, and the monument was not referred to for the time being.

"It will come up again," said one of the Isalle brothers, that evening, as everyone was going home at dusk, "when the old man dies."

9

Instead the old man changed his mind. He changed his mind when the miners hurled rocks at the Society windows and threw Roberto Manca's Veterans' Section poster into the river.

That was only the beginning. About thirty boys were involved, some of whom had not yet done their military service. They had left their work in the fields to go and earn a few more lire in the mines of Iglesiente. On Saturday night, with their pay in their pockets, they used to come back to town and, after a couple of drinks, imagine themselves lords of the earth. They were intoxicated by the rabble-rousers, who "filled their heads with nonsense," as much as they were by the wine. Bawling, they went up and down the streets. Out of tune they sang the "Workers' Hymn" and the "Red Flag" and another lament for the miners who died at Iglesias during the strike when the Vice-Prefect had ordered the Carabinieri to shoot them down. In this frame of mind they broke loose one night and smashed the windows of the Queen Margherita Literary Society and made off with the Veterans' poster.

The Veterans made a new poster and the "prinzipales" replaced the windowpanes and denounced the miners to the Carabinieri. Or rather the Commendatore sent for the Maresciallo and told him that if the incident were repeated he would have him transferred to an inland village. The windows of the Society were not broken again, but the following Sunday the boys from the mines began to go about town with red sashes under their jackets.

These sashes had not been worn for a long time, in Cuadu, and now that red assumed a particular, provocative significance. Those who did not wear a sash put a red carnation in their buttonholes.

In Cuadu lovers wear boutonnieres. The lover's message changes with the position of the flower and is tacitly transmitted during the Sunday promenade along the main street that runs through the town. But those carnations carried another kind of message. They were a threat, like the songs and the hymns that had never been heard before on those streets, in those piazzas.

The members of the Society exchanged meaningful glances and summoned the Maresciallo again. The Maresciallo said there was nothing to prevent people from wearing red sashes or carnations. Apart from that, what could a handful of Carabinieri do against the whole town? And the whole town seemed to be laughing boldly and celebrating a holiday, decked out in red carnations and red sashes.

In point of fact there were only about ten real rascals,

35

led by Baldovino Curreli. Earlier he had been a member of the Veterans himself, and had fought in the war. The voice in the night that cried out the names of the dead at Iglesias under the windows of the "prinzipales" was his. It was a stark, raucous voice, full of hate—wild, violent, and unmistakable.

"Arrest him for disturbing the peace after dark," said the Commendatore. But the Maresciallo could not arrest him, he had no proof of anything.

Then one Sunday something happened that induced even Monsignor Pau to intervene energetically with the authorities. At the end of the Mass a Socialist orator held a meeting of sorts in the Piazza, which left his listeners dumfounded. He spoke well, much better than the Monsignor, who was famous as a preacher. He spoke against the rich and the abuses of the rich, and the people of Cuadu were struck by the truth of what he had to say. Moreover it appeared, without once naming him, that he was railing against Commendatore Comina, who was standing at the door of the Society, leaning on his cane.

The crowd began to murmur, people turned to stare. For a moment the Commendatore almost lost his head and Dante Tavèra struggled to hold him back. The old man wanted to stand under the box and demand what right the orator had to say what he said—even he felt that the accusations were directed against his house. He would have heckled the upstart, hit him, had him arrested. Quite beside himself, he shouted that he too had lost a son in the war.

While Dante Tavèra and Gino and other members of the Society were trying to pacify him, Roberto Manca, with some ten of his Veterans—all men of about thirty with combat experience and ready with their fists—and a few students who were there on holiday, cut through the crowd and pulled the orator right off his perch.

There was an uproar. The students took to their heels while Roberto and five or six of his men were badly beaten up. The Carabinieri arrested one Veteran and some miners, among them Baldovino, but they let them all go immediately. The Maresciallo received his transfer by telegram.

It was after this episode that Roberto Manca, along with his comrade in arms, Antonio Dubois, and eight or ten of the others who had taken part in the free-for-all, founded his Veterans' League of Cuadu. And the Commendatore changed his mind and himself brought up the new proposal for the monument.

In the meantime the miners grew bolder than ever and from then on, every Sunday, they beat up the Fascists on the Vicar's Bridge until finally help had to be sent from Iglesias to lend a hand in Cuadu, where the boys with the red sashes were completely out of control. But all this occurred later, at the time of the famous march on Rome. In fact it was on the very same day, so that afterward it was hard to say which march they were talking about, the one on Rome, or the other, which cost the lives of Baldovino Curreli and the old Socialist, Felice Denise.

10

Things like these had never happened in Cuadu. A hundred years earlier the Lords of the State Council of Turin had promulgated the ill-famed Law of Enclosures and had taken away from the agricultural island communities the land that for centuries they had held collectively and cultivated under a system of crop rotation, between grain and forage. By force of law a myriad of small freeholders was created who, in a brief space, had had to sell their tiny holdings to the great landowners or to the speculators. The whole population rebelled and rose up and the leaders of the revolt were hanged behind the Church of Carmelo. But there were no hymns or symbols or banners or rabble-rousing sentiments. Again, during the war, when the women opposed the requisition of grain from Cuadu by laying themselves and their children across the railroad tracks, it was the same—no hymns, no red sashes, no light dawning in the East, or anything of the sort.

But now, for the first time, they were up against something that could not be resolved within the town itself, even with all the force of law and order. Useless to talk about secession and commerce with France and Spain if no one in Cuadu, not even the least citizen in his hut at the foot of Linas Mountain, could live in peace. Commendatore Comina, thinking of what was happening on the Continent, felt the wind at his back; he drew closer to his own kind, and to the tycoons from the north who had not, thank heaven, been idle. Even in Cuadu all those who had something to lose were of the same mind, so they rallied together around other symbols and other flags.

It was the Commendatore himself—no one else would have dared to mention it again—who proposed the monument for the second time. But he declined the Chairman's position on the Committee, although it was conferred on him by general acclaim. He wished—a noble sentiment, which everyone appreciated—that the job should go to the Marchese Manca di Tharros, already President of the Veterans' League, and of the National Marksmen's Association, and, as of a few days before, Secretary of the Fascist League.

As for the Commendatore, he tried to get used to the wake of D'Annunzio, to the death's-heads, the black shirts, the fez, the poniards, and the hand grenades, all the damnable things that had usually set him off into such a rage. Meanwhile the elementary schoolteachers were mobilized, and the young ladies of good family, and the students who had run away on the day of the oration, and, in small groups, protected by the Carabinieri and by the Fascists, they began to collect funds.

11

Thus it was to Pietrina Cherchi that Mariangela Eca gave her eight hundred and thirty-five lire, wrapped up and knotted in a handkerchief, just as she had brought them from the house of her priest.

It was only a few days after the girls had started going from house to house, and when the schoolteacher untied the handkerchief and saw what was inside she could hardly believe her eyes. She counted the silver, the notes, the small change, and then she was sure that there must be some mistake. No other offering had been anything like so considerable. The Commendatore himself had given two hundred lire for the whole of his family, and that seemed quite a sum. Others who were prosperous gave fifty, or thirty, or twenty, or ten lire, no more. The poor, in general, never gave over two or three lire, and some even less, or nothing at all. Possibly Mariangela had gone the rounds of her neighbors, but even that was unlikely.

She put the bundle deep in her purse, tied a blue silk scarf around her head, and went off in search of the Chairman of the Committee, to confide her misgivings and ask his advice. Eventually she found him at the Society, called him to one side, and whispered the story in his ear. But Roberto Manca, ignoring her entreaties, summoned all who were present and loudly proclaimed the news. The schoolteacher could do nothing but lay the handkerchief full of money on the cloth of the great table.

From the Society the tale spread through the town. They talked about it everywhere, repeating, word for word, the Chairman's letter of thanks to Mariangela Eca, which, dictated on the spot to Pietrina herself and read to the assembled Committee, had moved the ladies to tears. That a poor old woman who had already given both her sons for her country should then deprive herself of so much money, put aside at such cost, without a word, was deeply touching. It was an example that one humble creature had set for those who, despite the ease and comfort of their station, had limited themselves to finding a little loose change in their pockets. After the foundation of the Fascist League, Roberto Manca had recovered his eloquence.

But the letter, various copies of which were already in circulation throughout the town, was never sent, although it had the unanimous approval of the Committee. Old Comina, this time without shouting, expressed himself most judiciously.

"This foolish woman," he said, referring to the generous donor, "has no idea of the value of her money. She has given it by mistake. If we, who can read and write, accept eight hundred and thirty-five lire from a poor illiterate, it will be an outright swindle."

"But both her sons were killed," Roberto said.

"My dear Roberto," said the Commendatore, "people

are waiting to see what we're going to do with this money. And there's only one thing to do with it—"

"Give it back to her," said Dante Tavèra.

"Precisely," said the Commendatore, and on this note he departed, waving good-by to Roberto in such a way as to provoke some dutiful laughter.

Roberto Manca wanted to resign immediately, but Dante Tavèra and Gino Comina drew him apart. What, couldn't he see it was all a hoax? That money never belonged to old Mariangela, it came from Father Coi, who had worked out this diabolical trick to make fools of them all.

"A clerical trick," said Dante.

Thunderstruck by the evidence, Roberto conceded the fact and said nothing more about resigning. He took the Commendatore's sage advice and rewrote the letter. From Mariangela they would accept only five lire. They were returning all the rest. The words of thanks, the encomiums that had been baptized with such tears and enthusiasm, stood unchanged. But the same words, the same expressions, took on a fine sarcasm once they were really intended for the priest.

Once again he read the letter out loud and everyone approved of it. Then he licked and neatly sealed the envelope, which was addressed to the "Gentile Signora Mariangela Eca" and meant for the priest, in fact. Then, the better to speed the missive on its way, he made a very vulgar sign, for which he immediately apologized to the ladies present.

12

That was how it came about that Mariangela saw her money brought back to her by the same schoolteacher to whom she had only just given it. The girl had quietly explained to her what was in the letter so, without even opening the envelope, Mariangela put it and the money away in the bottom drawer of the bureau, which she could lock. Then she sat down all alone in the kitchen and set herself to thinking the matter over.

If she were willing to give them her money, why wouldn't they take it? Why did they go from door to door if it weren't money they were after? It was too much to fathom. In other circumstances she would have gone to the priest for an explanation and asked for his advice. But since she had acted all by herself it was too late to go to him now and admit that she might have been mistaken.

She could hear him snorting and coughing outside by the wall. Perhaps he was blowing his nose that way, like a trumpet, because he already knew that Pietrina Cherchi had returned her money. But he was not going to get it again. She had got her hands on it once and for all and it was not to be put back in the savings account. There had been no mistake. None at all. She would keep the money and very slowly, five lire at a time, she would succeed in making the Committee accept it.

Little by little they would take her money. She wanted

to give it away and never hear another word of it. And she would have no sermons or reproaches. Couldn't she figure things out as well as anyone else? According to the schoolteacher, they said she didn't know the value of eight hundred lire. But she knew! And how she knew! She had no use for all this nonsense. Perhaps she had been wrong to give the whole thing at once, when it was so much money. She should have given it bit by bit, just as she had made up her mind to do now. All she cared about was that the monument should be put up soon, that there should be no more talk about it.

Why, she wondered, did people talk so much? Their voices bothered her even from a distance. They drove her up the mountain, to that silent and deserted place where she lit the candles in the shed by the sheepfold, and warmed the coffee in the pot that she kept hidden along with the rest of her things.

Voices bothered her and the noises of the workmen and all the other sounds—the carts that passed, the clap of the horses' hoofs, even the rasp of her husband's hoe, there in the garden—all that bothered her.

13

She took the sickle, the long leather strap that she used to bind the bundle of wood coming home, she took an empty sack which, folded like a hood, protected her head and shoulders while she was carrying the heavy load down the hill, she took the little jar of olive oil for the lamps, the ground coffee, a twist of sugar, and some matches. When she was ready she said good-by to her husband, but she called out to him from the road so that Don Pietro too should know that she was going up the mountain. Old, crook-backed Girolamo turned and made a sign that it was all right, that he had understood.

Through the town she went at a jogging clip, a kind of dogtrot that would bring her to the sheepfold in just under an hour. As usual she hurried past the Piazza Frontera, hugging the wall on her way down toward the Vicar's Bridge. There she turned left along the river, then back up through the Castangias quarter until at last she left the voices, the confusion, the hubbub of the town behind her. Avoiding the cart track that wound up the mountain, she cut across the fields in a straight line, going through the thorny hedges like a stoat. Once in the woods she knew the paths that only the goats know. She kept going at a jog trot, anxious to arrive at that clearing, once lively as a camping ground, now silent, without bleat or cry, to be there in that great space at the deep valley's head, where Saverio had been buried for four years.

There, four years before, she had found him sitting, waiting for her, on the threshold of the shed—that surviving son whom the Company Commander had given up for lost, whom she had believed dead. She had come upon him suddenly where he sat, just as when he used to make the cheese, with the same smell about him. He was there, in front of her—not a phantom risen up from the earth, not a soul from purgatory, starving for expiatory prayer—but alive. And she had been good, she had been ready to imagine the thousand unutterable dangers and hazards through which he had fled from the front where his brother Giovanni had died, she had understood that he must hide himself there, in the shed.

She had been good, she had helped him, protected him, kept him alive for that little while which fate had left to him. But it had been a struggle against fate itself. Saverio had come up there opposing his lot, or trying to escape from it. She had understood that later. At the time she had obeyed him blindly. Quick and silent as thought she had done everything he asked her and agreed that it was for the best.

First she went back to town and got the priest from the church. It had been right to do that. Doesn't one call a priest when someone is born, or dies? And it was the same as if her son had been new-born in that instant. Or, if his fate were almost settled, he was in danger, on the point of vanishing, of dying.

She had called Don Pietro, she had begged him to go up to Baddimanna, to the sheepfold which he knew since he used to stop there from time to time, in the days when he went hunting. While she was talking to the priest she never mentioned Saverio. She did what she was told and spoke of "someone" up there on Baddimanna. But Don Pietro had looked her in the eye and he had understood. It seemed hardly possible that he had when she herself at that very moment, pleading for "someone," had begun to doubt the reality of what she had seen. By that time she was doubtful, even of her own self, no longer sure of anything.

Still Don Pietro had understood, he had read it in her eyes just as if he had been expecting it, and he had put on his hunting boots and gone directly, without waiting for her. And for that little while that Saverio had to live, for five days she had fought against destiny, and only she and the priest had known the secret.

Now, every time he saw her going away with the sack and the leather strap, Don Pietro knew where she was going, and what she was going to do, and he knew that the bundle of wood she would carry home on her back was just an excuse for the pilgrimage. He knew why, every autumn, she took rushes or a bunch of raffia, he knew with what care she repaired the shed and reinforced it against storms, while the rest of the sheepfold went to ruin. He knew about the little bottle of oil and the matches that she took to light the wicks that floated over the bottom of the glass.

Saverio had wanted to lie where she had found him when one day she went for wood, and he was buried in the shed where he had spent the last five days of his life. Nearby there were still traces of the fires that he had lit. The snow and the rain had not yet obliterated everything; a black circle remained where the autumn grass grew tallest.

Mariangela, in her memory, fixed him in that place, at the threshold of the triangular door, sitting with his legs apart, just as when he used to work the cheese in the copper kettle, with his sleeves rolled up above his hairy forearms. She could still hear his voice hailing her from the distance, as soon as he saw her, calling her "madixedda," which means wagtail, on account of her nimble, hopping gait. Life was all joy when her two sons were there in the sheepfold, in spite of the fact that the young one, Giovanni, was mean by nature. And how Saverio used to laugh, how happy he had been!

But the last time, sitting there with nothing in his hands, his filthy shirt in rags, his soldier's jacket over his shoulders, he had looked at her without a word, without telling her anything she wanted to know—how he had managed to get there, what had happened—without a word. They might have seen each other only a few hours before. Then he had sent her to get the shotgun and to call the priest.

Not lost, or dead, like his younger brother, but as if he were twice dead and gone, he had been there, a deserter (he had used that word, which she heard for the first time in her life, but the sense was not new to her), a bandit, someone whom the first Carabiniere who happened by could shoot on sight.

He had made her promise to tell no one that he had come, not even his father or his wife, and above all he did not want the doctor. He had made her swear on the memory of her other son. It was nothing serious, only an attack of malaria, he said. And he would not lie down on the bed of boughs inside the shed, nor let her light the fire.

She had carried out his orders, she had done all he wanted. She had run to Cuadu, free from her usual heavy burden, she had gone to the church to find Don Pietro, she had returned with provisions—bread, cheese, olives, wine, cigarettes—and the double-barreled shotgun, dismounted in two pieces and wrapped up in a blanket with the ammunition. For the second time she had taken the path back through the woods, carrying the bundle on her head, stepping quickly, almost running. But when she arrived Father Coi was already there, beside her son. She had had no idea what he needed to say to the priest that was so important and so secret, he who never went to confession, not even at Easter. But he had had something to tell him, important, and very grave.

14

Not even afterward did she learn what it was.

The boy was lying on his side, propped up on one arm, and Don Pietro was kneeling by him. With a sign he made her understand that she was to wait, to stay where she was, and she stopped and stood, stock-still, with the little bundle on her head. The priest was bending over, one knee on the ground, his elbow resting on the other. Every once in a while he took his hand from his forehead in a familiar gesture of deprecation, shook his head, acquiesced.

Mariangela had never before seen a man confess under such circumstances. For her the confessional belonged to the shadows of the church, to the grating that hides the face, through which the low voice repeats its burden. It seemed to her that she had come too soon, that she was in the way, but at the same time she did not dare turn back.

When the boy had finished what he had to say he stretched himself out on his back, exhausted, and covered his face with his hands. She saw that he was shaken with sobs, while the priest was deep in prayer. Those sobs of her son tore one unthinking cry from her. Then she began to whimper, like a dog, quite unaware of herself until the priest turned on her with a peremptory frown. In silence she continued to cry, blinded by tears.

After a little, when she could come close, she took

her son in her arms, cradling him, holding his heavy head to her breast, and the priest withdrew and went to the edge of the clearing while mother and son comforted each other without words.

Presently she began to set out the provisions—bread, wine, and tobacco—on the old cork shelf, suspended from a rusty wire. Then, promising to come and stay with him the following day, she fled, at a long, loping gait, to overtake the priest. But she heard him calling her again, "Mammài! Oh, Mammài!" and she ran back to him.

He had pulled himself up from his pallet and was kneeling in the embrasure of the door, loading the shotgun.

"Oh, Mammài, will he keep my secret?" and he pointed to the priest, a hundred paces away, who was gazing up into the branches of the trees, his hands in his pockets, his hat slung back at the nape of his neck.

"Certainly he'll keep it," she said, clenching her fists and stamping her feet. "Certainly he'll keep it."

But the boy was unconvinced. His glance went quickly from the priest to the shotgun, which he was holding open as he tried to slip the shells into the barrel. "Did I do wrong to make him come?" he said, looking at her with eyes dilated by fever.

"It's a secret of confession," she said. A few instants of silence went by. "Now go to sleep, my son."

Carefully she took the shotgun out of his hands and propped it up against the wall of the shed. She made him lie down on the pallet, she covered him with a shawl, and she felt him tremble. Without question he was the better of her two sons. Could there be any comparison between him and Giovanni? He was good, docile, where Giovanni had been brutal—a boy of violent words and gestures. Saverio, instead, was gentle, gay. What could have happened to him? How could he think of killing? And it was not only the delirium of fever—

She stayed a little while to watch him. He was shaken by chills which repeated themselves, but at longer and longer intervals. Perhaps he was already asleep.

Swiftly, with her light rustling, she overtook the priest, and both of them went on their way.

15

They took the road home together, exchanging a few words—the fever, the quinine which he would procure the next day and she would come to fetch—nothing more. But she felt that Don Pietro was cognizant of a grave secret that she would never know, although already it had become part of her suffering. Every once in a while she glanced at him, furtively. He walked, long-strided, absorbed and frowning, from time to time repeating that deprecating gesture with the same hand that, shortly before, he had lifted to bless and to absolve.

A little way from town they separated, agreeing to meet on the following day, for the quinine. Mariangela watched him as he went and then she turned off the road and took a few steps into the woods, glad to be alone. She leaned against a tree, pressing her shoulders hard to the trunk, dizzy and lightheaded—tricked by weariness, she thought to herself, breathing in deeply the humid air of the wood.

She could hear the priest's steps going away, down the road. His heavy boots crunched on the gravel and creaked on the occasional rocks. Through her clothes she felt the sharp shoots from the tree trunk stinging her shoulders, and the hard, thorny leaves at her back, but all this made a part of the lightness and the joy. It was something that had never happened to her, or perhaps it had happened, long ago.

She thought about it. Yes, once, years before, she had happened to be joyful as she was now, and there had been no reason for it. Rather, she thought, shaking her head and propping herself up against the tree trunk with one hand, it had been a happiness against reason. And now she had nothing but reason to cry, and she felt happy. Perhaps her head was ceasing to function properly.

She went farther, where the wood was deeper. Delight pervaded her, a warm rush of blood made her hearing more acute, sharpened her vision, revived her memory. With a pleasant sense of emptiness in her stomach she tore a twig from a bush and chewed it, deliberately enjoying the harsh, bitter taste. It was a wild joy, a stolen joy, and she would have to hide it from everyone if she were not to be treated like a fool, when she came home. She would have to hide it just as she had hidden it when she was still a girl, before Girolamo married her, and she had known that she was pregnant.

There, that was when, time past, she had experienced something similar. Just then. She had known that she was pregnant and she had carried the child secretly in her womb, without saying anything to anyone, that child, Saverio, who was up there now in the shed, sleeping.

Profoundly happy, she drew another breath. "Oh! Oh! Oh!" she cried out loud, clasping her hands and looking, through the branches, at the shining sky of sunset. At the first morning light she would go back up the mountain, she would stay with him all the next day. Perhaps she would find him still asleep. She would make him coffee, over the little fire of twigs, next to the shed, she would warm the pot of milk.

16

For five days the fever lasted, and this secret joy. For five days it had lasted, burning, consuming her soul. She went every day, sometimes twice a day, to bring him food, cigarettes, medicine, to make him coffee, to watch him sleep. She obeyed him in everything. She did not call the doctor because he had forbidden her to do it. In truth the boy kept the loaded shotgun beside him and warned her that if the doctor came he would stretch him out. But even without this threat she would not have defied him. It was important not to disobey him in anything. She knew how precious were those days, how she must keep the harmony they shared between the two of them—she, crouched beside him, he sleeping with his head against her feet. He needed her, next to him. Then his sleep was tranquil. When he was alone he was alert for all the noises of the woods, awake to the silence of the night. The days went by. Five days. She felt them going. Remembering it, afterward, it seemed to her that she had always known how many there would be.

17

The morning after the fifth day she found him outside the door of the shed, sitting on the ground, his shoulders against the doorjamb, the shotgun on his knees, the early light shining on his face. His eyes and his mouth were half closed, as if he slept in the heat of the first morning sun which was just showing itself over the crest of the mountain. But she knew instantly that he was not asleep. She understood it before she put down the basket, before she touched him.

The days were over, those numbered days. What was bound to happen had happened, what she had been sure of all along. She set the basket down carefully, she touched his forehead, as one does to feel a fever, she felt the iciness within, the cold of all that night, the stiffness, the definitive absence. Then, kneeling, not in blind desperation but consciously with arms flung open, she cried out to him, calling him with all her strength. In the name of all the long, silent agony to come she blasphemed and cursed the Lord's name. Ever after she remembered those terrible words which were stopped in her memory as if they had never come out of her mouth. But they were hers. She had carried them within herself always, against that moment that had to arrive. From the beginning everything had been predestined and now there was her son, guiltless before her.

Between his fingers she put the rosary which she kept deep in the pocket of her skirt, and then she went to call the priest again so that, with his holy water, he might silence the echoes of those words.

18

At first, each time he heard her go out and call to her husband that she was going "up," by which she meant to the mountain, Don Pietro used to reconsider all that had happened more than four years before when she had come to summon him to the sheepfold on Baddimanna. Then, as time passed, he was reminded of it only when he heard her voice from the house next door, a harsh, unexpected voice, like the squawk of a magpie.

Earlier he had thought of it almost uninterruptedly, taken up by the memory of it and the questions that he felt he had never definitely resolved. Had it been right or not what he, a priest, had done? At the foot of the gallows a priest may absolve a man condemned to death; he is called to absolve him by the same ones who have inflicted the punishment. But has a priest the right to help a guilty man escape the sanctions of the law? Has he the right to help him to escape? To hide himself?

When Mariangela had come to call him, that distant day, to tell him that "someone" needed to confess, someone who was waiting for him in the shed of the sheepfold, he had been certain that it must be Saverio, as in fact it was.

A thousand thoughts, a thousand possibilities pass through a man's mind. Everything under the sun may suggest itself at some time or other and then, when something surprising happens, it is precisely the thing that is most incredible, least probable, which we seem already to have perceived or divined.

When he looked back on it perhaps Don Pietro too felt that he had guessed the truth. In fact, while Mariangela was speaking, he had thought immediately that the person up there might be Saverio, although it was ridiculous to suppose that a man declared missing for a month should now turn up on Baddimanna. Still this absurd idea, once it had taken shape in his mind, provoked others which again remained unanswered.

Was it possible for a soldier from the battle zone to arrive at Cuadu—having crossed the whole of Italy, then gone by sea, embarked at Civitavecchia, disembarked at Golfaranci—to accomplish all this without being caught? Because if it were Saverio up there, it was clear that he had deserted. No, probably it was only his fancy, something suggested perhaps by Mariangela's bearing, or just by the look in her eye. What was far more likely was that Mariangela meant him to understand Saverio, but that she had had a hallucination, that the "someone" on Baddimanna was the creation of a mind obsessed with the memory of this last, lost son, a vision prompted by solitude and the silence of the woods. Were that the case, he would bless the shed and the whole, ancient sheepfold with the magic ritual to which he sometimes condescended when people believed that a place was haunted by spirits.

Again, it was conceivable that Mariangela's "someone" might be the bandit, one Pruneddu, who used to hang around the area and had once made himself at home in the Ecas' sheepfold for several days, but on the whole he inclined to the supposition that her mind was wandering—a feeling that was reinforced during the two-hour trek it took to get to Baddimanna in his heavy boots, with his mountaineer's stride.

In the end it was Saverio himself whom he found on the mountain. Coming into the darkness of the shed, he had been aware of a litter of branches and the acrid smell of fever, while the shepherd's rough, hot hands had taken his in a grip of iron. When his eyes had grown accustomed to the shadows, he had recognized the thin, bearded face lifted for mercy and forgiveness. It was then that he had had the sensation of having known, from the first moment, that the person of whom Mariangela had cryptically spoken was Saverio—a man alive by a miracle, whose very presence uttered the mystery itself of death.

Afterward he could not get out of his mind the image of that kneeling man who wanted him, was calling him, saying that he had come from so far away because only Don Pietro could help him. He had made him lie down on the pallet, he had stayed beside him, holding his hand to quiet him, he had promised to help him, and then Saverio lay silent, shaken by chills.

From long experience of people in trouble, Don Pietro could foresee the facts, anticipate the telling, and before Saverio began to speak he was already considering what must be done for him. He needed a doctor, he needed medicine, and, for the moment at least, it was necessary not to obsess him with the idea of what might happen— the military tribunal which he could not escape, the sentence, the possibility of execution. Perceiving these things, Don Pietro had decided at once that he would take care of him at all costs, and protect him, and even keep him hidden. He settled all this in his heart, but not without a furious rebellion against himself, so that later he had much to meditate upon. Still, he was glad to have made up his mind before he knew the story. He had decided to defend the deserter, whatever the danger involved, risking all there was to risk in doing such a thing.

19

Like a child Saverio had let himself be calmed, and although he was still shivering with fever he could speak. Together they recited the Creed, Don Pietro patiently helping him with the words that he stumbled over and repeated. *"Credo in unu Deu Patre Onnipotente,"* said Saverio, with a great effort. At one point he stopped and clutched Don Pietro's hand. His story could wait no longer. He must tell the priest why he had wanted him there. But Don Pietro had firmly liberated his hand and had made him go on to the end of the Creed. Then he asked him how he had managed to escape.

During an attack, said Saverio, he had stayed behind, pretending to be dead. He had hoped for an Austrian advance; he would have let himself be taken prisoner. But the Austrians had been halted, pushed back, their trench captured, and an enemy bombardment had begun again, which had made it impossible even to recover the wounded. He had made his escape through the gaps in the barbed wire that he and one of his comrades had made the night before. (The two of them had been sent to blow up the outwork because they knew how to smoke cigars as the Sardinians do, holding the coal in their mouths so that no glow was seen.)

Before he had got behind the lines he had thrown away his identification disk and every document he carried, and stolen another disk from one of the dead. By that time his fever was so high he could hardly stand up, but someone had given him a lift in a truck. In a way the fever and the delirium had saved him. He remembered a field hospital, a bed, nurses, an ambulance, and a vast railway station. He remembered walking in the rain along the railroad tracks, but whether inside the station or out he could not recall. Certainly he had done quite a piece on foot, but the longest stretch he covered in a cattle van, or a supply truck. All along it was the fever that protected him, not the identification disk that he had taken.

Together with hundreds of others he had arrived at Civitavecchia on a troop train. The convoy had been stopped before coming into the station and he had jumped off because the Carabinieri were examining all documents, so he had hidden himself again.

How he had managed to embark he did not know, nor

could he recall any part of the crossing. It seemed to him that he had always traveled on foot, or by train, or by truck. In the month that had passed since he had thrown away rifle and cartridge case there had also been a voyage by sea—embarkation at Civitavecchia, disembarkation at Golfaranci—but he had no memory of it whatsoever. It was as if someone had picked him up and transported him from one place to another without his knowledge, while he slept. A month had gone by. But he had been there in the shed for several days.

Don Pietro questioned him further, and from the replies, sometimes clear, sometimes confused, he pieced together a picture of the journey. Much was left unanswered because there were many things that Saverio had forgotten. All the same Don Pietro tried to understand, co-ordinate, and tie up the story: the roadblocks, the Carabinieri, the sentry posts—he had passed through every obstacle as if he were a ghost. His flight resembled the disappearance of one of those flocks of stolen sheep that thieving shepherds lead through valleys, over mountains, leaving no trace, with the skill of a prestidigitator making a coin vanish.

Not until he saw that he was answering all the questions calmly did Don Pietro ask him why he had fled. His account of this was entirely clear.

"You remember my Company Commander?" said Saverio.

Some time ago there had been an exchange of letters between Don Pietro and Captain P. in regard to Saverio's request to be discharged. The priest remembered the letters perfectly, and the captain's promises to expedite the matter.

They had not given him his discharge, Saverio said, but through no fault of the captain's, who had done all he could, though it had nothing to do with him. Still, the discharge never arrived and Saverio went to pieces.

"I couldn't take it any more, Father Coi. I'd had it."

Now he was talking calmly, clasping his hands between his knees, with only now and then a chill. He was unable, he said, to make himself go any more and "take prisoners," for half a pack of cigarettes or a slug of grappa, nor could he go and detonate the explosives. He and one other had always done the job before but by that time he was fed up, and the captain knew it.

Nevertheless, the last evening, before the attack, he had gone again, partly to show that he could do it if he wanted, and partly to spite the sergeant, and all the rest of them. Already he had fever and he felt drunk, although he hadn't touched the grappa that had been given them.

"I'm not making excuses, Father Coi."

He stopped and pulled himself up by digging his elbow into the ground. Slowly he shook his head, with his eyes closed. After a little he began to talk again.

20

Later it seemed to Don Pietro that he could remember what happened as if he had experienced it himself.

With one blast of the whistle the captain had got them out of the trench all together. He used to carry a whip, not a pistol like all the rest, but an oxhide thong. If, during an attack, one of them hesitated, he got a lash across his knapsack. It had a psychological effect, he would say, and laugh. Or, if one of them clung to the earth when he was not wounded, the captain would take him by the straps of his knapsack, lift him off the ground, and hurl him forward. He was tall and strong, he knew how to command, and his men loved him.

That day it was difficult to advance. The machine-gun fire drove the soldiers back like dead leaves before the wind. Still, little by little they were pushing on—now going ahead by leaps and bounds, now taking cover, now springing forward at a sign from the captain, pausing on the last stretch just to draw breath, before rushing into the enemy trenches.

At a certain point, during a charge, Saverio had seen the fiery spit of a machine gun and he had thrown himself down on his stomach, sure that he could hit it and knock it out. With his elbow on the ground, the wet stock of the rifle against his cheek, he was taking aim, holding his breath, when the captain's whip sang through the air, like a shell, and caught him behind the ear. It was the same old harmless, psychological whip-cut, un-happily misdirected; but while a bullet may be nothing, in the heat of such a moment, a whiplash is an outrage.

"I let him go four paces and I fired. I shot him in the back of the neck, Father. I saw him die. He spun around, flung out his arms, and fell."

With these words he stopped and they remained for a long time without speaking, Saverio on the pallet of branches, Father Coi bent over him, one knee on the ground. The story was finished.

Among the trees at the back of the clearing Mari-angela appeared, with the little bundle on her head. Don Pietro let her come within twenty feet of them before he stopped her with a sign. Suddenly he was convulsed with grim amusement. He shot one severe glance at the old woman from the tail of his eye.

"No," he said to himself, "you're not untimely. At least you've come."

Her arrival brought him back to the real situation, restored things to their proper perspective. How other-wise would he have been able to listen to the man and absolve him? In coming to him, all that Saverio sought was absolution, to be free of the burden of that death. He held himself responsible for a happenstance which, like the rifle bullet, had stricken him too. Responsible for something that had been part of the battle, only an-other aspect of the madness that left no one untouched, not even those who had not wanted the war, and who were involved in spite of that.

The old woman was waiting, standing still, with her bundle. As yet she knew nothing. Perhaps she would never know the real reason for her son's desertion. Perhaps in part she blamed herself for his pitiful state because when he had gone away she had pleaded with him to come back, to come back—

How could he, Father Coi, sinning and prone to frailty and compromise, lazy and cowardly in the face of the crooked world, how could he judge a man who was ready to accept the whole responsibility for an act performed almost automatically, but for which he held himself accountable as if he had done it with cold and calculated determination?

In fact it had no substance, that error for which, according to the laws of men, a man must be shot in the back. The soldier who was lying at his feet was not responsible for the death of Captain P. any more than he, Father Coi, was responsible for it. The sacramental formula that he was about to pronounce would apply, not so much to the crime of which the boy believed himself guilty, as to all the sins that dwell in human nature —sins to which Saverio was giving no thought, at that moment, but which were written, all the same, on his face. From these he could liberate him, as once he had rid him of worms.

"Repeat the Act of Contrition," he said, with his characteristic roughness.

Saverio had forgotten it. He had stopped going to church, he no longer went even to the Easter confession.

He was one of those who unceremoniously called Don Pietro "Priest Coi." He lay back on the bed of boughs, wrung with sobs, and covered his face.

The priest recited the Act of Contrition for him, keeping one hand on his forehead.

21

When he got back to Cuadu they were already ringing the Ave Maria and he went immediately to the church, still in his hobnail boots, which clattered on the steps of the main altar. There were only a few people, fewer than usual. He was late and the next day the Monsignor would find a way to let him know it.

"He'll think I've gone hunting again," he reflected.

In the days when he went hunting he always used to arrive late for the evening service. Once he had brought the shotgun and the game bag into the sacristy. A violent argument with Monsignor Pau had ensued.

"It is not fitting for the clergy to go about with firearms, to shoot, to stain their hands with blood," the Monsignor had said.

But it is good to walk alone with a dog, through the valleys, on the ridges of the mountains, the shotgun on one's shoulder, to lie waiting among the reeds.

"This time it would be a horse of a different color, if

he knew what I'd been up to," he muttered to himself as he was going back to the sacristy, followed by the altar boy.

Monsignor Pau was not there to take him to task, but he always knew everything sooner or later. Someone would tell him that Don Pietro had been on the mountain. But no one would ever know what he had gone to do that day, and he would never tell. Could he say that he had gone to fulfill his calling as a priest? That he had been sent for by "someone" who needed to confess? Could he say that without offering any explanation? No, he couldn't. Pride apart, it was too risky; no one would have believed him.

Let them think that he'd gone hunting, that he'd returned to his ancient "vice," that he couldn't resist it. Everyone knew the Monsignor's views on that.

But would his superiors have approved of his behavior if they had got wind of it? The Monsignor, or the Bishop of A? For the first time this simple question occurred to him and the answer was—certainly not. Perhaps the Bishop would have listened to his reasons, patiently condescended to let him talk, but in the end he would have said that Don Pietro's attitude could not be condoned.

"However," he said aloud, as he came out of the great church door and closed it behind him, "nobody knows." No one knew, outside of himself and Mariangela, that Saverio was in the shed of the sheepfold.

In the distance before him, behind the chapel, the

black bluff of the mountain lifted itself to the deep, still transparent blue of the sky. And no one in Cuadu knew that a man was there, shaking with fever. Beyond the roof of the chapel, beyond the smoke that was rising from the chimneys, lay that dark, silent mass from which Saverio, unseen, could see the lights of Cuadu.

"His eyes are like the eyes of a bird," said the priest to himself, as if he were reciting a verse from the Psalms.

Perhaps the fever had passed and he was waiting there among the folds of that dark mountain with the shotgun on his knees. Perhaps he was thinking of coming down, going home to his mother or to his wife, who knew nothing about it, so far.

"If he comes down, if he gives himself up, it solves everything," thought the priest, letting the heavy church-door key slide into the bottom of the pocket of his gown.

But Saverio would not come. He knew that perfectly well. He had looked back at him from the distance and seen him leaning against the doorjamb, with the black gun. And where had he got it, the priest wondered, now that he thought about it. It was always kept in the shed, like the copper kettle, like the baskets for the cheese. But it couldn't have been there, by the sheepfold, all that time. Mariangela must have brought it to him from the house.

No, he would never come down, nor give himself up. He was not like a bird or a young fox. He was armed. He had not put his faith in the mercy of the Lord, but in the aim of a loaded shotgun. And he had already killed a man.

Don Pietro felt a sense of uneasiness, almost of disgust, as he remembered Saverio's words. "I let him go four paces—"

The same thing could happen again. If anyone unwittingly were to go near the shed, if someone were to pass that way and see him—someone not a priest bound to the secret of the confessional—Saverio would let him go four paces and would fire, like the last time.

He shouldn't have left him with the gun. How was it possible that he hadn't thought of it, at the moment? Wearily he lifted up his hand, took off his hat, and let his arm drop slowly. "I'm a fool," he said.

For a little he stood there thinking it over, then he pulled himself together and turned toward the pharmacy, which was still open. After giving it a glance to be sure that the usual evening gossips were not about, he went in and asked for the quinine and the aspirin that he had promised Mariangela.

Although the pharmacist asked no questions, he felt impelled to tell him that the medicine was for a poor wretch who was receiving no help from the town. This unnecessary explanation brought back all his misgivings, sharper than ever.

22

Going home he saw that there was still a light in Mariangela's kitchen window, but he did not call her. He
closed his door, shot the bolt, threw his hat on a chair,
changed his shoes, and put the little pot of leftover soup
over the spirit lamp that he used to heat coffee in the
morning, when he came back from church. If Mariangela
had come and knocked, he would not have let her in.
Perhaps even the man in his shelter of boughs had lit
a little fire and was eating.

While he was automatically pouring the soup into the
dish, he was thinking of the shotgun. "Saverio always
took it," he reflected. "It's company, in the country."

He cut himself a large slice of dark bread and began
to eat slowly, like the peasants, as he went on thinking.
He poured himself a glass of wine and took a swallow.

Very likely Saverio hadn't killed anyone. When the
captain fell before his eyes he assumed that he had shot
him, that the bullet was his, when in fact it must have
been fired by the machine gun.

"He can't lie to himself. No, he can't do it," said
Father Coi, aloud.

He was dipping his bread in the boiling soup, to cool
it, and every so often he took a sip of wine. He poured
himself another glass.

"It was done in anger," he said. "Taken by surprise,
we jump, we react. It happens to all of us. The fault lies

with those who want war, and with those who don't know how to avoid it. We must oppose it," he said, thumping his fist on the table. "But in these days who is against it? Who?"

He cocked an ear. It seemed to him there was a rustling outside the door, perhaps Mariangela, barefoot, come to see if he were still awake. But while he listened all he heard was a beetle in the wardrobe. Still, Mariangela might have come as far as the door and heard him talking to himself.

"What can we do to prevent war?" he said. "Even if we wanted to do something, here in Cuadu what could we do?" His thoughts returned to Baddimanna, to Saverio in the shed, to his miraculous escape. If he had only fled and thrown away his rifle, without killing anyone . . .

Again he thought he heard the shuffle of steps outside the door. He got up and went to see, but there was no one. Beyond the garden hedge Mariangela's window was dark, the night without a moon. A sooty tangle of trees rose here and there over the darker shapes of the houses, massed together, and from the garden came a breath of damp earth. Slowly he shut the door again, and bolted it. In the morning, well before sunrise, Mariangela would come knocking for the medicine that he had promised. It would be better if he took it to her now, himself. That way she wouldn't bother him again.

Then he remembered some woolens that he kept in a trunk—two sweaters, past wearing, a scarf, a knitted helmet—and he went to light the lamp in the next room, which served him as a study and an office. Seeing it on the desk, he was reminded that he had not finished reciting the Breviary. No matter. He looked about for the trunk in the place where it had been for many years, although he knew it was no longer there.

The walls of the room had been whitewashed and decorated with rustic plaster moldings, and the trunk, where he used to keep his hunting clothes, was gone, as was the shotgun, the cartridge case, the game bag which had hung on the wall, and the little machine for making shot. The room, which one could enter directly from the street, had become the plain, tidy office of a priest, with the chairs lined up against the walls, the shelf of books, the sacred images, the little table with the registers and papers. But for all that the change had been made some years before, he always forgot about it when he went to look for something. Now the trunk was in a dark room at the end of the corridor.

He went into his bedroom to fetch a tallow candle, lit it, and in a moment he found the sweaters, the scarf, and the knitted helmet. He wrapped them in a newspaper, redolent of mothballs as they were, took the package of medicine and went out, bareheaded, leaving the door ajar. The damp night air made him want to smoke. He crossed the vegetable garden, opened the little gate that gave into his neighbors' yard, and as he walked in he thought, "I have never come through this gate."

In fact it was the first time in many years and it

seemed strange to him. At Easter he always went out by the street door.

Although the light in Mariangela's kitchen was out, his knock was peremptory, as if to say, "Hurry up, I'm here." Even if it had never happened before, who else but himself could it have been?

There was a stirring in the dark house, then a light at the window, then Mariangela rushed out, alarmed and half dressed. He gave her the bundle of clothes. He told her how the medicine should be given to the sick man, and watching her huddle in her shawl while she listened to him closely, he thought again, "It's the first time." But everything that was happening to him that day was happening for the first time.

Before he went away, to explain his coming at that odd hour, he said that he was going to A in the morning, that he was leaving very early.

"Tomorrow evening come and tell me if he still has fever, and we'll see what we can do." He spoke in the brusque voice he used with her and went off without so much as saying good night.

But the old woman's voice followed him, speaking almost to herself, saying, "The Lord will reward you." He slammed the door and shot the bolt, this time decisively. The dampness of the night had got into his bones.

23

He had left precise instructions for the care of the sick man, he himself had brought the medicine, the sweaters—

He was overdoing it. When someone is in trouble he must be helped. Very well. But he, Don Pietro, was overdoing it. He was exceeding his duty. During the day, however, had he not been called on just for that?

He tried to remember his state of mind as he had listened to the confession. He heard the words again, saw the bowed head, and it all came back to him, just the way it was. He had absolved Saverio even before he had finished speaking. He had entrusted him to God's mercy.

"It's easy," he said out loud, searching for a cigar in his pocket. Then he sat down, resting his elbow on the table, blowing out great puffs of white smoke. "It's too easy," he repeated, meaning that it was too easy to appeal to God's mercy.

He would have liked to explain everything to himself in plain terms, as if he were rendering an account to someone else. He remembered that before absolving him he had decided to help Saverio, before he knew his crime. But were there not two different things here—Saverio's responsibility toward his fellow man, and the mercy of the Lord?

"That's the rub," he thought, getting up and lighting the cigar again. "To make the distinction. To distinguish the one from the other." To understand, to dissipate the clouds from his mind, he must try to separate them.

A priest may absolve the gravest sin. But how can he help a murderer escape the law? In helping Saverio to hide himself he was helping him to flee from justice, he was making himself a party to the crime.

"I was so sure I was right. Why was I so sure?" he said aloud, trying to concentrate.

Something was eluding him, something that once he had grasped. Not some proverbial truth, tucked in a formula, but something within himself, something that Saverio had given him, which could restore his confidence.

He went to get the Breviary from the study, opened it, and began to read. *"Ostendit mihi arborem salicem tegentem campos ac montes—"* but after a little while only his eyes and his lips were following the familiar words.

Twice Captain P. had replied to his inquiries about Saverio's discharge. The letters were still in a drawer. He opened it and found them right away. In a rapid, engaging handwriting the captain wrote that Saverio's discharge did not depend on him. He had nothing to do with it, it was a bureaucratic affair. However, he would do everything he could by turning in a good report on the soldier. He referred to him as "the fine boy from Cuadu," and "your dear godson."

Saverio had passed himself off as his godson—a misrepresentation that he, Father Coi, took care not to contradict.

In the second letter the captain advised him that he had written to the Ordnance Officer of the Brigade Commander, who had promised to interest himself in the matter. Very likely Saverio would be able to come home to Cuadu. It was dated a month and a half earlier. A few days later the fine boy had shot him in the back of the neck at four paces distant. "I saw him die. He spun around, flung out his arms, and fell."

He put back the letter, closed the drawer, and began to read again from the beginning. *"Ostendit mihi arborem salicem—"* He read it to the end, recited the evening prayer, undressed, and went to bed. But in the dark the doubts that tormented him became even more oppressive. Had it been a mistaken sense of pity that had induced him to promise help and protection to a murderer? Pity, not persuasion? He lit the lamp and sat up in bed, shaking.

Suddenly a resolution of these difficulties occurred to him. In the morning he would go to A in fact, as he had said to Mariangela. He would start early and talk to the Bishop. He would put his trust in him. Of course he would not have the Bishop's approval, but he might clear up his own misgivings and cast off his burden.

Although it was late at night he rose, put on his shoes and his gown, and laid out the clean linen, the fresh clothes that he would wear in the morning—in a few hours—to go to A. From the wardrobe he took his buckled shoes, his cloak, his beaver hat, which he wore only on great occasions. Then he went back to bed and slept.

24

Well before his usual hour he woke, with a start, lit the lamp, and saw the linen and the clothes laid out for the journey. He opened the window and in the dark he narrowed his farsighted eye to read the time by the white clock face on the bell tower, above the rooftops. He washed his face, rough with beard, and made a lather to shave himself. The considerations of a few hours ago now seemed to him both unreasonable and ridiculous. The whole thing was perhaps not so serious, so irreparable and final as it had appeared to be in the solitude of the night.

While the sky took on a cast of green the dark silence was slowly slipping away, but the noises of the town were still isolated and distinguishable, one from the other. They told him that he was not alone, that he could reflect calmly, that he had time. The empty truck, which was waking distant echoes, passing over the cobblestones with a deafening clatter, helped him to think. He had all the time he needed for meditation on the things that, the evening before, had seemed so intricate, insoluble.

Who was accusing Saverio of killing the Company Commander? No one. No one was accusing him.

"He is responsible to the Lord. No man has asked him for an accounting," he said to himself, grimacing at the mirror. He did not like his own face.

But why had none of this come into his head the night

before? The Bishop would have to resolve the matter, would have to decide. It would be interesting to see how he got around it.

Whenever the priest put on clean linen, sweet-smelling from the wash, it was always a keen pleasure, but he hated to lay his everyday things aside and dress himself in the clothes that were kept in reserve for feast days or ceremonies. Nevertheless he got dressed. He felt rested and lightheaded, he felt strangely like laughing, and he was curious to hear what the Bishop would have to say. At the same time he was aware of a profound tranquillity which he knew was irrational, since it proceeded more from outer circumstance than from within himself.

"But I'll go, I'll explain how I was called, what I did, what I said," he remarked, and twirling the great cloak in the air, he put it over his shoulders.

Dressed to the nines, Don Pietro went out, shut the door, and slipped the key under the step that had been its place for years. By now it was day. No longer green, the sky was streaked with violet. Distinctly he recollected the thoughts of the night. They had come to seem logical and absurd, like a geometrical theorem. As he stood watching, the black of the mountain was growing rusty. He imagined the noises of the distant wood—the deep, sly rustlings, squeakings, whistles, barks, voices—dissolving in that empty air where the birds poised themselves, and the silence that came after. Turning, he sharpened his gaze on the clock face of the bell tower. There

was time, plenty of time for the train. He crossed himself and went into the church, as on every other morning.

25

When he had finished saying Mass and had left a note
for the Monsignor, he strode rapidly toward the station,
which was a quarter of an hour's walk from the center
of town. He had gone almost halfway when he was over-
taken by a rickety trap that came to a stop as a familiar
voice hailed him. It was his old friend, Urbano Castai,
the local doctor at Ruinalta, who came to Cuadu from
time to time to get slips, seeds, and young plants for his
orchard from the Comina nurseries. Now, tied at the
back of the trap, he had some ten small orange and tan-
gerine trees whose green tops were waving behind his
head.

"Get in," said the doctor, gesturing vehemently. Don
Pietro got in and the doctor whipped up the old cob,
who arched his tail and set off at a brisk trot, pulling
the trap down the hill with an ear-splitting racket.

"You're going to miss the train," shouted the doctor,
driving like a jockey, with his knees apart.

Don Pietro, who was hanging on to his hat with one
hand, gestured, as if to say, "It doesn't matter," while
the doctor made a fist at him, shook his head, and kept

80

up the pace. The wheels were wobbling and sending a spray of stones and gravel into the hedges.

"I saw you in the distance and I caught up with you," shouted the doctor. "Where are you going?"

The priest cut the air with his free hand in the direction of A, the seat of the Bishop's palace. Pulling a long mouth, the doctor looked him in the face. Dressed like that, where else could Don Pietro be going, if not to the Bishop? He glanced away.

"Have they summoned you again?" he said, with a short laugh. His mustache was lopsided and yellow from tobacco.

They arrived at the station five or six minutes ahead of time. The little locomotive was maneuvering, giving out quick, childish toots and emanating the acrid smell of the coal from Bacu Abis.

"Thank you," said Don Pietro, turning to look at his friend, but he was in no hurry to get out. "Thank you very much."

With his handkerchief he flicked off his robe and his hat, trying to brush away the dust that in the brief stretch of road had inundated him and even settled on his eyebrows, which were thick and black. He passed the handkerchief over his face and looked closely at his friend.

"How do you happen to be here today?" he said.

The doctor was watching him, scrutinizing him sharply. His hazel eyes, tranquil and ironic, had stayed young in his fat, aging face. "I came to get these," he said, waving his small white hand at the little plants tied to the back of the trap.

Don Pietro, who had gathered as much, nodded thoughtfully and laid his hand on his friend's shoulder. He had not yet decided to get down. "What's the hurry about seeing the Bishop?" he was thinking.

"Thank you for the lift," he said finally, "but as a matter of fact they haven't summoned me and perhaps it would be better if I put off this trip. Perhaps it would be better."

"They haven't summoned you?"

"No, they haven't summoned me. Where are you going now?"

"If you were leaving I'd go home. But if you're not leaving I'll take you back to your house. You can give me some coffee."

"I'll go your way for a piece, if you don't mind," said Don Pietro, staring at the callus from the pruning shears on the palm of his hand.

The doctor observed him narrowly. "You know what we'll do?" he said, gathering in the reins and pulling up the cob's head. "We'll have coffee at my house, and this evening I'll bring you home. I still have that wine you liked—"

Although he laughed, his hazel eyes were serious and watchful. He had turned the horse around and was about to slap him with the reins but he held off for a moment, looking at the priest as if to say, "What's going on here?"

Don Pietro smiled and clapped him on the knee. The horse took off like a rocket with the rattling old trap, so that the two men had to steady themselves by clutching the mudguards. Only by shouting could they make themselves heard, such was the din.

26

Urbano Castai was as famous for his eccentricities as he was highly regarded as a doctor. Immediately after taking his degree he had been assistant to the chief surgeon of the Hospital of Santa Restituta, who also lectured at the university. Many of his former classmates remembered him as a young man, standing at the operating table next to the professor, who treated him more like a colleague than a disciple. Everyone was sure that he would take over when the master retired, but suddenly the young surgeon gave it all up. He turned his back on the university, the hospital, the professor, and accepted the practice at Ruinalta where he had remained ever since, and grown old. Many years later, in medical circles, people still talked of that brilliant career so arbitrarily interrupted. He was felt to have been most unwise, momentarily touched in the head.

But Urbano Castai himself had no regrets. He had married a rich man's daughter, become the father of half a dozen children, went hunting when he pleased, and devoted himself to his fruit trees. In recent years he had set out his orchard, which was one of the best in the region. He continued to be an excellent diagnostician and his old colleagues called on him for consultations even in the city, but he did no more surgery except in emergencies.

Malicious rumor had it that his hand was no longer steady, since he had taken to drink. It was true that he drank, but the charge was unfounded. In his own view a surgeon was a specialist whereas he was still a tyro, hence he had stopped. But when it happened that he had to operate, he was as good as ever. In Cuadu and in Ruinalta everything was laid to the bottle, his brilliance as well as his oddities, but no one had anything against him, bar one or two big shots who disliked his political leanings.

It was said that he was an anarchist, an atheist, and a materialist, none of which was true unless one takes the word "anarchist" at its most vague, imprecise, and unhistoric meaning. Urbano Castai was a law-abiding man who could not accept the law and order that had been established in Italy after 1860. He was the kind of man who went on dreaming, longing for another system, a republican, an uncompromising disciple of Mazzini. But that was enough to constitute him as an anarchist for the members of the Literary Society of Cuadu or of Ruinalta. In fact he was a Tuveriano, as he often reiterated, and not without a touch of malice. Giovanni Battista Tuveri had been a philosopher from Collinas, but his countrymen had long since forgotten him and his cause was lost. Nevertheless as a young man Urbano Castai and some of his friends had printed at their own expense a posthumous work of this obscure thinker, *On the Rights of the People to Overthrow Bad Government.*

Now, however, the doctor's civic activities were limited to the administration of the Monte Granatico, the little farmers' bank whose capital he had managed to increase to the unheard-of sum of one hundred and fifty thousand lire. Politics was a thing of the past, of his youth, something to which he had come to refer with detachment, with a certain skepticism. Only after he had been drinking could he rekindle this ancient passion.

His name as an anarchist, enemy of governments, priest-baiter, skirt-chaser might have been explained by certain of his sudden rages which the good people of the town had no difficulty in relating to the "Filu Ferru" or the Malvasia that he poured down his throat. Far and wide they thought of him as all those things, and not even his old friendship with Don Pietro contradicted this opinion in the least.

Don Pietro was the only priest he tolerated. He thought of him as a man like anyone else, the only one he had never been able to scandalize. Their friendship sprang from their school years. Nothing had changed it, neither differences in profession nor in habits of mind. After school was finished each one had gone his own way, but they never lost sight of each other. They talked, they argued, they went on long hunting trips together during which they sometimes hardly spoke at all.

What they had in common, to judge by appearances, was only a passion for hunting, a love of gardening, and an innate aversion to city life that had led them both to bury themselves in two such small towns. But when they were alone they still argued with boyish vigor, and the burden of their discussions would have been incomprehensible to the people among whom they spent their lives. Without recourse to the "Filu Ferru" or the Malvasia they talked of books, politics, religion, or, in a calmer vein, of the orchard, the garden, the Monte Granatico of Ruinalta.

Whenever the doctor came to Cuadu to pick up young fruit trees, or slips, or seeds, he never failed to go and find his old friend, who usually made him stay for lunch. Don Pietro always returned the visits, when he could, but his own were less frequent once he had given up hunting.

In any case it was not the first time that together they were taking the road that winds around the mountain and joins Cuadu to Ruinalta, but some years had gone by since they had done it last. Every so often Don Pietro, shouting above the racket of the trap, would ask his friend about the changes that attracted his attention along the way—a gate rehung, trees that had grown to top the walls, forming an avenue, a vineyard, an orchard, a cottage sprung up where there had been a gravel pit. He asked the news of this or that landowner, this or that farmer—who had gone to war, who had died, who had come back, instead, from France or from Tunis. All the improvements had been made toward the end of the war, when prisoners' labor cost only a few cents a day and the growers who had stayed home had been able to take advantage of the situation.

The farther they went from Cuadu the more scattered were the gardens and the orchards. The countryside became more solitary, with only a few meager olive groves or vineyards closed behind hedges so high they seemed to suffocate the piece of ground and the vines they protected. Finally there was nothing but a bare, sloping moor covered with a uniform expanse of brush.

While the horse went on at his brisk, bandy-legged trot, the two men, shaken up by the jolting carriage, fell silent, and Don Pietro's eyes wandered across the heath to the foot of the mountain. It was a long time since he had had the pleasure of finding himself in deep country at that hour of the morning. In the distance the rusty green of the broom and heath became a thick, downy fleece, a soft, continuous flowing that broke off where the vegetation stopped and stones broke through the lumpy, reddish earth. How many times he had crossed those clearings! How many miles he had done on his long legs from the mountain to the plain, from the plain to the mountain, following his dog! How many rounds he had fired, how many hares and partridges had swollen his bag.

As they went on the blue profile of the mountain unfolded, assumed different forms, each one well known to Don Pietro. Looking at those humps, those spurs, those saddles, those dwarfed black trees like cloves, which appeared, thrust upon the slopes, and slowly receded from his view, he knew just how it would be a moment later. But if he let his eye travel along the flank of the mountain everything seemed new to him. He did not remember having seen those cascading heaps of rock, those shadowed clefts, those precipices, those eagle's peaks. Was it possible that he had never noticed this savage aspect of the mountain, that he had never been aware of it before? The poor, desperate trees with naked roots that clung to the river of stones which filled the gullies had left no trace in his memory.

He put his hand on his friend's arm and indicated the mountain. "Was it always like that?" he said.

"What?" said the doctor in astonishment, and stopped the horse.

"Like that—a desolation?"

The horse twitched and his master slackened the reins to let him stretch his neck and crop the grass at the roadside. For a while they sat without speaking, gazing at the overhanging mountain, still stunned from the racket of the trap. The doctor lit a cigarette and Don Pietro took a half-smoked cigar from his pocket.

"Do you think," said the priest, breaking a long silence, "do you think it would be possible to prescribe for a sick man without seeing him?"

The doctor studied him again, trying to understand what was behind the words, the real question.

"You, for instance," Don Pietro went on. "If I described the symptoms could you take care of him?"

"Who is this man you're talking about?" Urbano said brusquely.

"It's someone— It makes no difference who it is. Could you do it?"

"That depends," said the doctor, annoyed. He shook the reins and the horse gave a start and took off again suddenly, at his bow-legged trot, rousing a flight of sparrows.

"You're asking strange questions," the doctor shouted. He slowed the horse to a walk and said, "Where is this man?"

Don Pietro gestured vaguely at the mountain.

"And you think you can take care of him keeping him —leaving him outdoors?" said the doctor, looking severely at the priest.

"I asked you a question and you haven't answered it," Don Pietro said.

After a long silence the doctor pulled on the reins and the horse came gently to a stop. "Are you speaking of someone who has no choice but to stay up there?" he said, jerking his chin at the mountain.

The priest made a sign of assent.

"Forgive me, Don Pietro. I'm a fool," said the other, thoughtfully. "We've known each other for years, one word from you should be enough. But I was slow, this

89

time. The fact is you're strange today. I keep trying to guess what's got into you instead of listening to what you tell me. Forgive me. This fellow couldn't come to me?"

"I'm afraid not," said the priest.

"If he could come to me—not to my house, naturally —but did I tell you that I'd bought a piece of land up there? Look, do you see that rock? No, that one—" With the handle of the whip he pointed at the mountain, the whole, crumbling, naked mountain. The priest pretended to have understood.

"Now let your eye travel straight down," said the doctor. "See where that flight of doves is rising? There, there in back of that bluff, that's where my land begins. I paid hardly anything for it, and there are almost sixty acres. I made a killing. If your man would come there— if he liked— There's a cave that's dry and protected. I could take care of him. I go up there every day. I'm grafting the olives. I'm doing it with my own hands, a little at a time."

Don Pietro clutched his friend's arm, by way of thanks. How much better he felt already! He was glad to have met him, come with him, talked to him.

"Look," he said, struggling to conceal his emotion, "I was really only asking for reassurance—to get an idea of what I ought to do myself. But perhaps this man isn't so very ill, after all. Perhaps he'll get by with it, on his own. I don't know if he has malaria or something else. I wanted to ask you about it and certainly if you're willing to help him, take care of him—" For a moment he was silent, then he went on. "You see, he's entrusted himself to me, and only to me." He made a great effort and added, "As a priest."

Again they were silent. Don Pietro was bent over, fitting his finger tips together, relieved to have spoken to his friend. Urbano did not even know who Saverio was, nor had he asked. Whatever happened he would certainly not betray him. Moreover, the real secret, the inviolable secret, was another thing entirely, and it would remain inviolable even to this man who could offer to help a stranger without a moment's hesitation. The only duty of a doctor was to heal the sick. That was all.

27

They spent the rest of the day together. A little before noon they arrived at Ruinalta and Don Pietro, according to established custom, waited in the kitchen with the doctor's wife and daughters while the doctor was seeing patients in his office.

After lunch, not in the trap but on horseback, despite the unsuitable clothing of the priest, they set out to follow the devious paths winding up to Urbano's sixty acres, his bargain. The ascent was steep and covered with enormous boulders. Scattered thickets of wild olives sprang up among the broom and the juniper.

"Once it was all forest," Urbano said. "But when the speculators from Tuscany came looking for coal, they timbered it clean—old trees, young trees, right down to the roots. Sometimes they didn't even leave the roots. Look at those holes! Still, they left the rocks. And the olives are coming up again. The birds brought back the pits.

"Do you know how many olives there must be? More than four thousand. I'll plant others, and in the meantime I've begun grafting."

Talking steadily he led Don Pietro up to the cave, whose mouth was hidden by brambles. Entering, they ducked their heads, and once inside Urbano touched a match to the newspaper he carried, illuminating the great cavity whose floor was covered with a thick, white layer of dry bird droppings.

"See those footprints? They're mine. No one has ever set foot in here."

The cave was warm and dry. When they left, the doctor pointed out to Don Pietro that instead of coming by the route that they had taken, one could also arrive from the opposite direction, by another road that scaled the mountain. In case of necessity the priest was to alert him by telegram, with some conventional message, whose text and possible variations they settled there and then. Either Don Pietro would bring the sick man to the cave, or the doctor would visit him in the sheepfold, if he were too ill to move. On the other hand the need might not arise, in which case, too, they would be in touch.

When they went back to Ruinalta Don Pietro took his leave of the Castai women, picked up the package of medicine that the doctor gave him, and without further words set off for Cuadu, on horseback.

On the way home he watched the profile of the mountain, approaching, receding, then slowly taking on its usual, familiar form once more. Later, from the courtyard of his house, he saw it again, immovable, its great cone closed into its black woods, full of darkness and nocturnal silence.

Mariangela came to give him the news of Saverio. She was happy as she had been years ago when she had come to tell him that the worms were gone. It was the first time she had been like that in a long, long while.

So it was for three more days. The old woman came, went, and returned to report. The sick man was better, the fever had subsided.

But the fourth day, at about nine o'clock in the morning, she arrived at the church distracted. Don Pietro must go, he must run! *They* needed him. Without another word she fled, without even genuflecting before the main altar.

28

He overtook her two hours later on Baddimanna. Girolamo and Saverio's wife, Lica, were also there. Fifty
steps from the shed, at the edge of the clearing, he
stopped to dry the sweat from his face. Outside the
door of the shed, where Saverio lay on the black wool
shawl, Lica was kneeling, rocking to and fro as she
wailed. Opposite her Girolamo was crouched on his
heels, and with a little twig he was keeping the green
flies that infest a sheepfold off his son's face. Mariangela,
standing, her head cocked on her shoulder, was doing
nothing and even later on she did not alter her stance.

When he had caught his breath again, Don Pietro
went closer, sure by now that he saw what he had not
expected to see. He had not imagined this death, he had
thought he was needed for advice and comfort.

Lica, hearing him approach, had begun to howl
louder than ever. Sobs and a singsong chant mingled
with the howls, a long, modulated litany of blame, in-
terrogation, and praise of the dead. Why hadn't he
wanted to see her? Why had he kept her away? Why
hadn't he let her take care of him?

Don Pietro was filled with distaste for that lament
which seemed so familiar that he might have heard it
before. Girolamo got respectfully to his feet and si-
lenced the woman, who then began to sob softly. The
priest came nearer and stopped at the dead man's feet,

taking off his hat like anyone else. Girolamo too took off his cap.

The body was not straightened out to its full length. The knees were bent and the arms folded across the chest. Don Pietro looked away from the rigid, bearded face, looked around, looked up. White clouds were passing swiftly. And after all everything had resolved itself, although the end was different from anything he had reasonably supposed, different from anything he had foreseen. He, who had seen so many people die, had not been aware that Saverio was dying. In those days he had been thinking of him all the time and yet Saverio had died without his knowing.

Now the decision that he had made no longer needed to be justified, it was just. It had a logical justification that had not once occurred to him, since he had never postulated that Saverio was about to die. The rightness of his conduct was revealed by what had happened, by what was irrevocable, was revealed in the silence about him, where every word was superfluous.

For a long time he remained absorbed, as if in prayer. Then, with an effort, he pulled himself together and asked why they had dug the pit in the shed. He took them to task for it, but without conviction. He said they must bring him down to Cuadu and register his death, in the usual way. He said they must observe the regulations. He said all this in a hurry, to get it over with, but his heart was not in it.

Mariangela said nothing. Girolamo did the talking,

repeating what he had heard from her. In the last few days, when Saverio had seemed to be a little better— but that was only the approach of death and he himself had known it—he had made her promise not to hand him over to the authorities even after he was dead. He had asked to be buried there in the shed, and to be left there forever.

While he was speaking, the old man frowned at Mariangela. She was to hold her peace and not to cry, as if they were not talking about Saverio at all.

Then silence fell, as before, where words were useless, superfluous. Everything was clear, everything was understood without the need for words. Once Don Pietro had instantly decided that he would not denounce the deserter, that he would help him stay hidden. Now, as quickly, he decided to help his family follow his wishes, to let them bury him in the old shed.

He knelt and said the first prayer for the soul of Saverio Eca, who, for a whiplash, dealt by accident, in the heat of a battle, had killed his commanding officer— or perhaps had only imagined that he had killed him. As he entrusted him to the Divine Mercy, certain that Saverio had already largely expiated his crime, he hoped that he, Father Coi, was not committing the sin of arrogance.

29

At the moment he had had no doubts. Time passed, and the service which he had read deliberately, in conscious violation of his office, that revocation of the formal instruction which he should have been able to set against every doubt or retrospective uncertainty, began to torment him. By what right had he infringed the rules to such an extent? The absconding of a deserter, over whose head hung the threat of the firing squad, and that secret burial were two completely different things. What reason was there now to keep the secret to which he had made himself an accomplice, once Saverio was dead?

The war was over, the prisons were empty, the military courts disbanded. Principles, which earlier it would have been sacrilege to question, had become debatable, were tried in argument. What might once have been considered high treason was now, in some cases, looked upon as a vindication of rights, a social affirmation, an act of merit. There were deserters who had not only been rehabilitated but were holding public office, sitting in the Parliament. Saverio too, if he had lived, might have taken his place in the world, got a flock together again, pastured his goats on Baddimanna.

In the light of this Don Pietro thought it proper that his remains should be returned to the cemetery in Cuadu. At least it was logical. Thus one day, a few months before the young ladies of the Committee began to collect funds for the monument, he told Mariangela that he wanted to talk to her, and a little later she joined him in the church, at the time of the vesper service.

Don Pietro was already sitting inside the confessional stall, rehearsing, like his prayers, the things that he must say to her—the clear, cogent reasons that should induce her to do what he thought was right. He heard her lift the latch and come in, he saw the streak of light from the opening lengthen itself along the floor, he heard the familiar rustling cease, a few steps from the door, and as if he were leading her toward him in his mind he coughed to guide her to the confessional. Docile, she came, knelt behind the grating, and greeted him in the usual way, saying, "Jesus Christ be praised."

"Let Him be praised forever," he replied, in a hurry.

They recited the Creed together and then, instead of putting any questions to her, the priest began to speak, repeating in a low voice the things that he had prepared to say. He spoke quickly, excitedly, without the serenity proper to the interview. Everything he had worked out for himself, all the arguments that he had arranged in order of their importance, now seemed to him so much nonsense. He stopped and was silent for a moment, and behind the grating he heard the old woman's breathing and smelled her ancient odor of cottage smoke. Then she spoke, just as always when she confessed, in an impersonal voice, a kind of low monologue.

She said that she knew what a concession he had made when he blessed the shed and the earth in the shed. She said that she had always known that sooner or later her son's last rest up there must come to an end. And the end had come. Perhaps it was better that way. Perhaps it was just to bring him back to town, to put him in the cemetery, where all the others lay. If Don Pietro said that it was the thing to do, then it was right. Who would know better than himself?

Only one thing displeased her. It was not so much that the bones of her son should be removed, brought down from there, not so much that as that it would make talk, there would be talk about it. It distressed her that she would have to listen to all the silly questions they would ask her.

Don Pietro sighed with relief. She was not opposing him, she was willing, she was putting herself in his hands. Quickly he said, "Perhaps I was in error, Mariangela. If so, I should make it right. Perhaps I made a mistake—"

She thought for a minute and replied, "You were not mistaken. The Lord will reward you, Don Pietro."

They had said all they had to say to each other. The interview was over. All the same, the priest would have liked to go on a little. But he decided to dismiss her, and he told her to go in peace.

30

Every day Mariangela came to him as usual to do his chores. She seldom spoke, and in the few words they exchanged neither of them ever alluded to that conversation. It was as if she had simply gone to confess.

Time went by and Don Pietro let it go. Now that he knew that Mariangela was not against him, he was in no hurry. He had made up his mind to talk to the Pretore, instead of the Maresciallo of the Carabinieri, but still he did nothing about it.

The Pretore, who had been an officer during the war, was a young man, newly appointed. Whenever they met on the street he always spoke warmly to Don Pietro, as if he would have liked him to stop awhile.

Don Pietro knew exactly what should be said and what there was no need to say. He meant to tell Saverio's story and leave Captain P. out of it entirely. Long since, in his own mind, he had drawn a fine dividing line between what was part of the secret of the confessional and what was not. It was perfectly possible that the captain had not died by Saverio's hand. For the matter of that he might not even have died. Who knew but what Saverio, remembering, elaborating, in his feverish solitude, might not have invented the whole thing? In any case he, Don Pietro, had no right to mention it.

Saverio's story, if one reduced it to its legal essentials, might have had an outcome similar to that of the bandit Pruneddu, who, after having lived by his wits for many years, had made some nice recalculations and, without even the advice of a lawyer, had decided to return to everyday life by giving himself up to the authorities so that he could take advantage of the amnesties that had been granted in the meanwhile.

Don Pietro's mind was made up. He had only to lift a finger and the young Pretore, at a friendly sign, would take him by the hand, accompany him to the door of the church, and they would talk. All the same he was in no hurry. He let days go by, months.

Then one day the girls began to go about the streets of Cuadu with their shoeboxes sealed with sealing wax, and Mariangela asked him for the eight hundred and thirty-five lire, which she gave to Pietrina. After that they accused him of having given the money to embarrass the Committee and create confusion. And everyone fell to quarreling. And they had the first riots in the Piazza, with the broken heads, the arrests, the charges, the recriminations, even among the Veterans for whom the Fascist League of Cuadu had been founded. And then there were more riots and the Fascists in Cuadu got the worst of it, until finally help came from their comrades in Iglesias to put things to rights.

And thus a new era began for Cuadu—*a fascibus receptis,* said Monsignor Tarcisio Pau.

31

It seemed to Don Pietro, who had done nothing to enlighten them about the money, nor said a word to defend himself against the ridiculous charge that they laid to him, that he himself had not only taken part in all the confusion but, in a certain sense, had even had a hand in its making, if quite involuntarily. Several times he had thought of swallowing his pride and speaking out.

He talked it over with Urbano Castai, who gave his opinion shortly. The priest should have set them straight at once, faced them down, and treated them like the imbeciles they were. By now it wasn't even worth mentioning.

"You flatter yourself that you're responsible for everything that happens in the world," he had concluded.

"Not in the world, just in my parish," Don Pietro had replied.

In fact it was no longer even "his" parish, since the Monsignor had arrived in Cuadu, but he still felt responsible for whatever happened. If they beat each other up in the Piazza, if a charge of dynamite exploded under the house of a "prinzipale" or of a Fascist—the two had become practically one and the same—he felt that he had failed to prevent things from getting so far out of hand.

Reasoning in private, he convinced himself that he was arrogant and presumptuous, since even the powers invested in a priest have limits commensurate with the weakness of human nature. But his first impulse was always the same. When, in the middle of the night, a blast rocked the town to its foundations, he could do no less than fling himself out of bed and rush into the street.

In the wake of the echoes, rebounding like thunder, then losing themselves in the valleys, came the furious barking of hundreds of dogs. The first explosion occurred after the arrest of Baldovino Curreli, when the Fascists broke up the meeting of the Socialists. From then on, each time a miner was thrown in jail, a charge of dynamite went off in Cuadu.

Each "prinzipale" suffered in turn—the Mancas, the Cominas, Edmondo Escano, with part of a wall of his house blown away. But after a while the townsfolk took no more notice of it. The men stayed in bed with their women and no one walked around with a loaded shotgun any longer. They knew what it was all about and who was behind it.

Don Pietro, on the other hand, threw on his cloak and ran. He used to arrive on the spot before the Carabinieri, guided by the smell of the explosion. As luck would have it, there was usually more noise than damage. Those who underwent the reprisals had good, solid houses, and slept in the bedrooms at the back.

Who set off the charges, no one knew. There were suspects, but no proof, and the boys with the red sashes could leg it when they wanted. The Carabinieri set a guard at the street corners and worried citizens watched and waited behind half-closed windows, but it was no use.

Once even Monsignor Tarcisio Pau had his turn. The charge was bigger than the others, but as usual the damage was minimal. The front door was blown up and the windows were shattered.

"These terrorists must be shot!" thundered the Monsignor, in his nightshirt, with the same aplomb as if he were holding a conference.

Urbano Castai, who was a light sleeper, heard every blast. When he came to Cuadu he winked at this one, wrung that one by the hand, waved his arms and congratulated all and sundry, as if each loiterer in the Piazza were an expert with dynamite. If he met Don Pietro he slapped him on the back and cried, "You're a fine lot, you fellows!"

At Ruinalta there had been no explosions and the sleep of the "prinzipales" was quite untroubled.

32

Two pretty girls from Iglesias were guests of the Mancas at that time. Fanny was sixteen, Julia nineteen, both smart and quick with an answer. Their voices were loud on the street, they imitated Carmen Boni and smoked, and they cared nothing for what people might think—unlike the ladies and the young girls of Cuadu, who always maintained the strictest decorum.

As they were going home one night, a hundred feet from the Mancas' door they met a bunch of boys who began to sing the "Red Flag." Roberto was not with them. Fanny, with a foolish giggle, planted herself in the middle of the street and before Julia, the elder, could stop her, embarked on a Fascist song that had never been heard before in Cuadu—*"La Disperata eccola qua!"*

There was a burst of shrill whistles from the boys, then a stone bounced off the pavement and struck Fanny above the right eye. She made no sound but put her hand to her bleeding face. Julia let out a yell and all the street was in an uproar. The boys tore down the hill at breakneck speed in their hobnail boots.

After that the Fascists from Iglesias came to teach the miners a lesson.

They came on a Sunday. The Via Roma was full of people in their best clothes. There had been no fighting that day. It might have been any sleepy, tranquil, prewar Sunday.

They arrived suddenly. They left their truck behind the church, flung themselves in the midst of the crowd, and began to give chase to the boys with the red sashes. But it was Baldovino Curreli they were after, and they had flasks of castor oil to make him drink.

They went to rout him out at home. He was unarmed, but he whipped out his clasp knife and with his back to the wall defended himself as best he could. Five or six of them jumped on him and finished him off under the eyes of his wife and his two children.

33

The schoolteachers' drive for funds was a modest matter of direct request, and since the returns were also modest other measures had to be taken by Roberto Manca and his collaborators, some of them suggested by the most influential members of the Society. Not only money but grain, foodstuffs, household objects, and even barnyard animals were solicited. People were getting more generous, or less stingy.

With the Prefect's permission a "festival" was organized—it was the first time the word had been used in Cuadu—with contests for impromptu verses, lotteries, a slippery-pole race, a shooting gallery, and a Jack Horner pie. At Roberto Manca's insistence Monsignor Tarcisio Pau got the Bishop of A to send for Don Pietro Coi and persuade him, in a friendly way, not to make any trouble. Not unnaturally they feared that Don Pietro's famous objections might diminish the take.

But there was no need for Father Coi to point out to the housewives of Cuadu that they were getting back the very same objects that they had given a few weeks before. They could see it for themselves. Those who wanted the monument would have to pay for it. It had come down to that.

At the beginning of the summer Roberto Manca proposed to set up an open-air cinema. He had gone over the project with great care and the members of the Society had approved it. All during the season the theater was open in the inner courtyard of the elementary school. The plan had been extremely simple to carry out—a screen made from four sheets, a rented projector with films, and a phonograph, lent by Gino Comina. Every Saturday and Sunday, from dusk to late at night, the cracked voice of the phonograph repeated, *"E lucean le stelle, stridea l'uscio dell' orto."* Glinka's *A Life for the Tsar* was also a favorite.

But it was only the "prinzipales" who ever went.

That same autumn, first at the Society and then in the lobby of the Town Hall, a plaster model of the original project was displayed. Everyone went to see it. Mariangela went too. Small as it was, it resembled the white glass cheese-dish that one of her neighbors had won in the Jack Horner pie. It consisted of a little box surmounted by an angel, wings outspread, who was supporting a naked man with a helmet and the stigmata of Christ. Monsignor Tarcisio Pau explained the symbol from the pulpit, and praised the sculptor's work.

The following spring, with the addition of a conspicuous contribution from the township, the plaster model was translated into marble—a real monument that still stands, blackened by time, in the main square of Cuadu, with the seventy-three names of her war dead inscribed on the slab in bronze letters.

In all that time Father Coi had done nothing about talking to the Pretore, had not even lifted a finger. Over and above the logic of the arguments that had brought him to decide to bring the deserter's remains back to Cuadu, was a nostalgia within himself for those four years, a sense of regret—as if the grave had already been opened and the poor bones taken back from the earth that was consuming them. Right or wrong, it gave him pleasure to think of that secret grave. It was a restful thought and gave him the strength to bear the insinuations of the Deacon of the Seminary and the brazen taunts of Monsignor Pau, who considered the monument a personal victory. The remembrance of the solitary grave in the sheepfold brought him peace and one day, without saying anything, even to Mariangela, he came in his heart to a new decision. He decided to do nothing, and to leave the grave where it was.

34

———————

Mariangela was waiting, but as usual she said nothing. She was waiting for Don Pietro to make up his mind about what he was going to do, and at the same time, without impatience, she was waiting for the plans for the monument to be realized. Every now and then she went to put five or ten lire secretly in the collection box, which was placed in the lobby of the Town Hall beside the plaster model, and went on waiting. In the end she succeeded in putting all eight hundred and thirty-five lire there, without anyone's being the wiser, although it was only her money that was ever found in the box, not a lira more.

She waited for months, asking nothing of anyone, and at last she saw workmen, digging out the foundation and constructing the granite base. Then she ran for seclusion to the solitude of the sheepfold and lit the lamps in the shed.

The next day there were the steps and the dark marble slab with the names inscribed in bronze letters all around. Finally a huge truck brought the poor, wounded soldier and the angel, with its great wings outspread, and they were hoisted to the top. Mariangela stayed to watch, and when it was finished she asked a student to show her the names of her own sons. The boy traced them with his finger, and read them to her.

> *Eca Giovanni*, Sergeant
> *Eca Saverio*, Private

Then, after all that time, she cried, like any other mother—for no reason but that the names were written backwards, the last name first, as in the Town Register. That was what made her cry in the end.

The monument remained sheeted for more than a week

and then they unveiled it. There was a solemn ceremony with elaborate preparations, speeches, hymns, and she went away. They looked for her in vain. She hated speeches too much, she could not listen to these, even though she knew it was the last time. When they came looking for her Girolamo said she had gone to fetch wood.

Saverio's widow was at the ceremony, with her fatherless child. Seeing them, so neat and destitute, Don Pietro could not help thinking that if he had brought Saverio's remains to the cemetery, they might have risked losing their meager pension, in spite of the amnesty.

Mariangela came back late in the evening when everything was long since over. As always she had kept the lamps burning in the shed until she left, she had returned with the heavy bundle of wood, and when she had unloaded it in her back yard she went to see the monument.

There was the angel, wings outspread, in the evening light. Soon it would be dark.

No one was left in the Piazza. There was nothing but silence, just as she had dreamed of it, for so long. No vain or foolish words, only silence.

For the rest of her days she went on bringing wood down from Baddimanna and working for Don Pietro Coi. Between themselves they never spoke of the grave which she continued to tend and which, after her death, would be left to the silence of the mountain.